Ten Past Eight

The Contemporary Women Writers' Club

Lucy Cavendish
Miranda Glover
Rachel Jackson
Anne Tuite-Dalton
Jennie Walmsley

For more information about
The Contemporary Women Writers' Club visit
www.cwwc.co.uk

This book is published by Queenbee Press
www.queenbee.co.uk

A CIP Record for this book is available from The British Library

ISBN 978-0-9568053-0-0

About us

Ten Past Eight is the second short story collection from *The Contemporary Women Writers' Club*. The book follows *The Leap Year,* our well-received debut which hit Amazon's Short Story bestseller list in 2009. This time we've taken on a new challenge. Each story contains a 'climax' of one sort or another at ten past eight (that's 2010 for those who want the subliminal reference) on the night of the World Cup Final; one moment, twelve lives, many threads. All the main characters are women and what we didn't know until we wrote it, is that they all in their own ways prove themselves to be brave.

Writing to a brief like this one is a cornerstone of our collaboration. We find focus and freedom through sharing our work and developing new ideas together.

With the creation of Queenbee Press, our own imprint and www.cwwc.co.uk, our new virtual home, *The Contemporary Women Writers' Club* is now ready to expand from our small core to embrace all women who write.

Come and meet us there to share in our creative approaches and ideas; enrol on one of our creative writing courses or live seminars. Hear, see and read the views of the most established and respected women writers alive today. Share your opinions in our forums and debates.

We celebrate the publishing opportunities of this digital age. It offers writers community, voice and more routes to publication than ever before in the history of the written word. Come and join us and grow our community. We can't wait to meet you there.

Lucy Cavendish, Miranda Glover, Rachel Jackson,
Anne Tuite-Dalton, Jennie Walmsley

Preface

Rachel Johnson, editor, The Lady Magazine

I am sitting at my laptop. One boy is staying over with a pal in Oxford, another man-child is in a boxing gym on the Harrow Road, and the daughter is in her room, surfing ASOS.com for the new season's looks which all appear to involve expensive aviator jackets. My husband is watching a DVD called the Prophet. It is evening, ie it's after *The Archers*. I am on my own. When you're writing, that's the only place to be.

"What's the movie about?" I asked earlier, mulling over whether to join him with a glass of Pinot Grigio. I should add that we are officially "not drinking" after Tony Blair revealed in his monster memoir *A Journey* that a sharpener of a G&T followed by a half bottle of red constitutes "alcohol dependence." This officially makes me, editor of *The Lady*, a binge drinker, a proud claim that I suspect honourable members of *The Contemporary Women Writers' Club* – whose stories you are about to plunge into with relish – might also make for themselves. Forget *A Journey*! When it comes to real life, to the pleasures and anxieties and right royal pains in the arse that constitute middle-aged romance, family, children, holidays, friends and so on, you can't turn to the bloodless memoirs of a male politician. What you need is a woman, preferably a mother, who is desperate to restore her mojo through the magic formulas of fiction, and a generous pour of Cab Sav. And that is what we have here, times twelve.

A helicopter has just buzzed overhead, and keeps on buzzing, so I looked at the clock in the corner of my screen – a habit, in case the police come round and ask exactly what time, madam, I heard the shot ring out? And it says 20:10. I promise I am not making this up. All these stories, in case you hadn't realised, take place on the day of the World Cup final at ten past eight, hence the title. The miracle of planning and plotting that this must have required from the five writers makes me feel weak at the thought.

They have produced a collection of dazzling, dirty verve and dash. Once you start reading the stories, it's impossible to stop. It's as if you already know the characters – or as we say know, we feel the connection – and it's sad to say goodbye to them. I don't often feel that about characters in 120,000 word novels.

But it's now 20:16, and although it's not the day of the World Cup Final in my house, I have supper to cook, and you have to get on with these sizzling stories.

Content

Becky *Prayssac*

"There was something about Becky. It wasn't only psychological but physical. Clare had never been sexually interested in women but Becky made her feel charged, she had a way of talking that made you feel special, a way of moving around you that made you feel both captivated and captivating."

Miranda Glover

Becky Prayssac
Miranda Glover

Becky stood thigh deep in green water, narrow hips swaying in red trunks, boyish torso twisted so you could see one smooth breast, the protrusion of a nipple. Behind her the midday sun glinted sharply on the wide river. Her dark hair was cropped and her face was bright with challenge.

"Come on," she urged, "it's like silk. Let's swim to the other side."

Her friend Clare and Becky's husband Mark sat in shadow on the pebbly beach. Clare's husband, Liam watched her from the shallows where he was skimming pebbles with a toddler. The child wore nothing but a sagging nappy.

"We shouldn't leave the kids," Mark called to Becky. He glanced backwards at three more young children, clambering over the boulders that separated the beach from the car park.

Earlier the two couples had made their way down the path with food from the local market, children balanced on hips. The setting was dramatic; stony beach, broad river, limestone cliff towering over them from the other side. It was Becky's recommendation. She had been here before.

"Don't be so damp," Becky called to Mark, taking another step forwards. Now she was submerged up to her hips and had clasped her hands behind her head, as if performing an African dance. Clare noted that Liam had stopped skimming stones.

"I'm game," he called out triumphantly, "Go on, Tommy, back to your daddy."

Clare watched as her husband leant down and turned the toddler towards Mark, then started wading out to Becky. Now they stood side by side, his broad frame close to her narrow one, their bodies swaying slightly as the current beckoned them in. Becky took the plunge first, shrieking as her body cut through the water. She turned onto her back.

"It's delicious," she said, "Come on!"

Liam laughed and launched himself in after her with a splash while Mark hauled Tommy into his arms.

"I'd better change him," he said. "Need to go back to the car."

"I'll start getting the food out," Clare replied and stood up, but her attentions remained fixed on Liam's back. She was fearful of deep water, of the undercurrents. She wanted to call out to him but her tongue was stuck to the roof of her mouth.

"What's Daddy doing?" said Evie, throwing her small arms around Clare's legs, "That's very deep."

Clare stroked her five year old's auburn hair and together they watched. Liam and Becky were moving fast, dipping up and down like a pair of otters, their hair glistening in the glare of the sun.

"Daddy's a big boy," she heard herself soothe, "He can look after himself."

The river was wider here than where they had hired the villa a few kilometres away. Becky had commented on this earlier at the market, "And there are tall cliffs the other side, which you can climb," she'd added, "It's wild."

'Wild' was an adjective Clare was beginning to realise Becky favoured. "Nothing seems satisfactory unless it's more 'wild' than the last thing she's done," she'd reflected to Liam en route.

"Actually I think it's quite refreshing," he'd replied.

They'd been following Becky and Mark's car. Becky had been driving too fast around the bends. Liam was speeding after her, faster than he would normally choose to go and when Clare had asked him to slow down he'd said, "Relax," with uncharacteristic derision, then put his foot down harder on the accelerator, causing the car to swerve dangerously on a dusty bend.

Now Liam was swimming out with Becky having a 'wild' time while Clare stood on the beach, the children circling her like baby vultures.

"Where's mummy?" asked Becky's toddler, Joel, "Hungry."

It was nearly one but in holiday mode Clare realised that Becky's life was not controlled by the hands of the clock. If the kids were hungry it was 'character building', as long as Becky wasn't ready to eat, they didn't eat.

Clare began to unpack the picnic, giving each child a knob from the ends of the baguettes to keep them going. She took the knife from her rucksack and split the first one, adding slices of ham and cheese. All the while she kept one eye on the water. Liam and Becky had reached the other side. Becky was wading out of the river, distinctive in her red trunks. From afar she looked like an adolescent boy. Liam was just behind her. They were both breathless and laughing. Clare cut her knife through the second baguette.

Mark reappeared with Tommy. Clare handed him a sandwich with a doleful smile. Then they stood together in silence, watching. The light bounced bright on the water between them and Liam and Becky, who had sat down on the other side of the river, both faces raised at the sun. Their shoulders were just touching. Liam shaded his eyes and looked across at them.

"Daddy, Daddy!" called Evie and Bess excitedly, jumping up and down.

Liam waved back enthusiastically.

"Don't worry," murmured Mark to Clare, "It'll pass. It always does."

The air was thick and muggy. This morning *le Figaro* had forecast a storm. Mark had flagged it to the children as they sat eating pain au chocolats on the terrace – big graphic clouds and lightning strikes littered the map of South West France. Liam had just appeared, damp from his shower. Moments earlier Clare was sure she'd heard voices from the bathroom window above the terrace but when she'd asked Liam if Becky was getting up he'd said he hadn't seen her.

"Can't wake Beck until she's ready," Mark had said, "It's like stirring the dead."

"Mummy's not dead," Joel had said.

"No I'm definitely not. Did you say there's going to be a storm?"

Becky had appeared silently at the doorway to the kitchen in an old Rolling Stones T-shirt and a pair of Mark's boxer shorts. She had bed-hair and rubbed one foot lazily up and down the back of her other calf. It forced your attentions down the length of her bare, brown legs. Mark held up the paper towards her.

"I'm scared of thunder," moaned Bess, climbing onto Clare's lap.

"Don't be so silly," said Becky, taking the paper from her husband and sitting down. She bit off the end of a croissant, "Shakes the world up, so we can all begin afresh."

Clare felt jaded. On holiday she and Liam had agreed to alternate getting up with the kids in strict rotation. This morning Evie had woken at five. The heat had already been stifling. Clare had watched a whole DVD of cartoons on her laptop with her before anyone else had even stirred. Last night in bed she and Liam had talked about the differences between them and their holiday companions.

"I think he's afraid she'll leave him if he doesn't give her exactly what she wants," Clare had said.

"Maybe it's simply that he loves her,' Liam had replied. Clare had remained silent, understanding the implication. It was a culmination of the past few years, sheer exhaustion, his insatiable energy, ambition, desire for more of everything: sex, society, alcohol, adventure. She by contrast felt the kids had sucked her energies out.

Now Liam and Becky were back in the water, swimming across the river towards them. The sun was still bright on their faces. They looked renewed. Perhaps she should have thrown caution to the wind and swum out too. Stated her claim. Maybe that was what Liam really wanted her to do. Instead she'd thought of the children. She poured some wine into a blue tumbler and took a large sip, then poured a second one and handed it to Mark. They 'chinked' plastic.

"Time to take a chill pill, as Becky would say," said Mark with a generous smile. He balanced his cup by a rock and picked up a towel for his wife, then sauntered towards the water's edge.

For the next hour they ate and drank and watched the water drifting past them. The kids played with stones. Liam sat on the beach next to Becky.

"We have to climb up the cliff," she said between mouthfuls. "It's such good fun. See down there, the rope bridge, we can walk across it with the kids and they can all have a go."

Clare had noticed the bridge earlier. It looked worn and precarious. She waited for either Liam or Mark to protest, but no one spoke. She didn't want to be the one to say no, but equally she was not keen to see her five and seven year-olds trying to find their next uncertain footing. She glanced at Liam but he was avoiding her gaze.

As Clare cleared the picnic they began on their expedition, the children following behind. Even Mark was going. They looked like a jaunty circus troupe, Clare the sole member of the audience, sitting alone on the beach watching as they trundled across the swaying bridge. It wobbled with every footstep and she listened to their shrieks of excitement with increasing dread. The danger was plain to see and they hadn't even reached the foot of the cliff yet. She couldn't understand why Liam would put his own desires before the safety of their children. For a moment she hated him.

When she'd met Becky last year it had been a relief. It was as if this other woman who seemed so convinced of the sense of her life choices was an affirmation that she herself had also been in control of her destiny; their children went to the same school, they had both taken a career break to raise their families, they seemed to share the same politics, like the same films and books. They had soon become friends, dropping in on each other after the walk to the school gates for a coffee, sharing a joke at the expense of the world around them. Their lives had seemed to be following the same paths.

When Becky had invited them over for dinner that first time Liam had groaned, but agreed to go all the same, because it was what Clare had wanted. Much to his surprise, the evening had proved a success and made Clare feel more empowered than she had over the previous few years, when it had often seemed it was Liam who was calling the tune in their lives, she the passive partner at home, while he continued to develop his career, to bring the money in that made it all possible. Mark worked in the media too and he and Liam had immediately hit it off. Liam had seemed uninterested in Becky that night, more keen to get to know the man who was making his name as a media lawyer, someone he may be interested in doing business with over a lunch in the city's creative heart. That night she also knew that Becky and she had been more interested in each other than their husbands. There was something about Becky. It wasn't only psychological but physical. Clare had never been sexually interested in women but Becky made her feel charged, she had a way of talking that made you feel special, a way of moving around you that made you feel both captivated and captivating.

Looking back on it now, as she watched them all reach the end of the rope bridge intact, Clare realised that, that first evening, Becky had worked a strange magic, like some pagan spell. She had concocted all the right ingredients, bought organic lamb from the farmer's market, served it bloody, accompanied it with bottles of warm rioja and pre-rolled grass joints strewn casually across the table with the coffee like after dinner mints.

Liam and Clare hadn't done drugs since university, in fact had never been that interested in them, even back then. But that night they all had all smoked and afterwards danced to some obscure contemporary jazz, lights turned low. Becky had danced first with Mark, then Liam and finally with Becky herself. She had come very close, her hand on the base of Clare's back so it made her feel hot. Afterwards Liam and Clare had gone home and dispensed with the babysitter by cab, then made love on the living room floor.

From then on there had hardly been a day when Clare and Becky didn't speak, text or see one another. They shared care of the children after school and both began to work again. Becky was an 'abstract expressionist'. She had a studio in Willesden Green. Clare was a reference book editor and she began to take on manuscripts again. A year had passed this way, with more dinners, lunches, picnics in the park. And now here they were, two families joined Clare now realised, by nothing but circumstance, holidaying together by a dangerous river in South West France.

"Mummeeee!"

Evie's voice bounced across the currents like a flying fish. Clare stood up hurriedly and waved anxiously at her two children, running up and down the far side of the river. She watched as Liam gave Becky a leg up and she began to scale the face of the cliff in her bare feet. Next came Joel, then Liam, then Bess. Soon they were all clinging like limpets to the rock face, Becky rising like a lizard up the cliff, the others clambering up behind her. Clare ran along the edge of the river and up on to the rope bridge. She tripped, falling so that one of her legs caught between the rope's knots and hung below the bridge towards the water. She managed to pull it back out, scraping the skin so her shin bled. Taking it more slowly, she reached the beach on the other side. By the time she reached the bottom of the cliff they had all already made it to the top of the cliff and stood above her, waving down.

"Come on," called Liam, "It's really easy, you can do it."

Becky ignored her husband's calls, turned and made her way back across the bridge to wait for them in the car.

Later they drove back to the villa in silence. Bess slept all the way. Liam didn't try to cajole Clare and she didn't humour him. The humidity felt ready to break. After the kids were safely in bed, Clare took a shower and didn't bother to come back downstairs.

She woke early. Liam wasn't next to her. She imagined he'd risen to tend to the children but when she came downstairs the house was silent. As she moved to the terrace she saw him wandering through the fig trees towards her, wearing nothing but his shorts from the day before. He hesitated when he saw her sitting there, then grinned ambiguously.

"I'm going to take a shower," he said, "Then try to catch some zees." He kissed her on the top of her head, mildly, like a child. He was perspiring lightly, smelt fecund, almost like sex. Clare watched as he sauntered inside then she sat and waited.

One by one the children and then Mark rose. The heat made them all irritable. Her head ached with it.

"No wonder they're both still asleep," Mark said,

"They were playing cards till dawn."

After breakfast he took Joel and Tommy to the boulangerie in the village. Clare and her daughters sat on the tiled terrace in the shade and made a giant jigsaw of the *Mona Lisa* that was at the villa when they arrived. Eventually Becky appeared. She had dark circles around her eyes and was bare beneath a long, white cotton nightshirt.

"I wish the storm would come," she complained as she clattered around in the kitchen preparing coffee, then she sat down at the table on the terrace and leafed through yesterday's paper.

"Everyone seems wiped out by the heat," Clare ventured, "or did you all stay up late?"

Becky looked down at her on the floor and smiled. Her expression made Becky feel uncomfortable. Today she no longer knew or trusted her at all. Mark reappeared with the bread and the kids who were eating cornets; ice cream dripped down their chins and onto their T-shirts. Becky made no attempt to rise and help him clean them up. Joel was clutching his toy fire engine. He spent hours pushing it back and forth and back and forth across the terrace. Each time it whirred the lights came on and the alarm sounded. It was beginning to grate on Clare's nerves.

"Good news," Mark announced jovially, "They're showing the world cup final in the village bar tonight. They've got a massive screen set up and are serving canard-frites for anyone who comes. I've reserved us a table."

"Amazed anyone cares," Becky said.

"This area's full of Dutch," said Mark, "It'll be a great atmosphere. The locals will all support the Spanish, it'll be a bloody great showdown between them and the second- homers."

He had a problem with the car, and even though it was a Sunday, said he was going to find a garage. "There's no fucking signal here on my Blackberry," he said, "I'm going to have to take my chances."

It was a perfect excuse for Mark not to look after the kids. Clare didn't blame him for needing to take some time out. She wondered what he knew.

Liam didn't appear. She couldn't be bothered to go and wake him. Instead she made pasta for the children and they picked at it in the heat. The sky was beginning to thicken, the blue morphing to grey. Becky went for a swim and her children trailed behind her without invitation. Clare waited with Bess and Evie, promising they would join the other children once their food had gone down. Barely fifteen minutes passed and Becky reappeared, wet in her trunks, the children running along behind her complaining that she had not let them swim. She ignored their complaints, said they were going for a siesta, made them follow her upstairs.

During the afternoon the heat became unbearable. The light turned a mawkish yellow and the clouds thickened to a veil across the sky. After a while Liam appeared. He looked pale beneath his tan, hardly spoke to Clare and swam with the kids. A deep thud of reggae resonated from the house and when they came back up for tea they found Becky and Mark on the terrace reading books and ignoring their children, who were pushing the fire engine backwards and forwards across the tiles so its alarm sounded over and over again. The music was loud, Clare assumed, in an attempt to block out the noise from the toy.

She went upstairs and took a shower. When she returned Liam was cooking omelettes for the children. It was half past seven.

"We want to go watch the football in a minute," he told her, "So I thought I should cook for the kids now."

"Great," she replied, "What time do we need to leave?"

"Oh, do you want to come?" he asked. Clare looked at him and wondered why he would think otherwise. The last thing she realised she wanted was an evening here alone with Becky, who was still sitting sullenly reading her book.

"Of course," she replied, "After all it's too hot to for the kids to sleep."

It was true. The clouds were gathering but still there was no rain. The humidity had become intolerable. Liam shrugged.

"Well we have to leave soon," he said. "Why don't Liam and I go on ahead, grab a beer, and you girls follow with the kids when you're ready," suggested Mark. Becky glanced up.

"How 'bout you take the children," she retorted, "I need to take a shower and Clare hasn't had time to get ready. We'll meet you all there."

It was five to eight by the time they left. Becky had gone upstairs. As she watched the backs of her husband and children wandering up the road towards the village Clare heard the first roll of thunder. Large droplets of rain began to drip from the sky like glue.

"Go quick," she called out, "get the kids inside." Within moments the droplets had turned to a cascade and lightning was striking across the skies like live wires. She shuddered at the thought of her children running through it, but it was too late to stop them.

Becky reappeared in a short red dress. She was wearing matching lipstick that made her look like a doll. Her skin had turned swarthy in the sun. She switched the reggae back on loud and grinned at Clare as if sharing a secret. She was holding a glass of wine in her hand.

"I love storms," she said, "They make me feel alive. Let's dance."

It was as if the coming of the rains had washed Becky's tension away. She began moving around the terrace, swinging her hips and laughing in a way that made Clare feel nervous. She wanted to ask her, "Did you fuck my husband last night?" but the words wouldn't come. Instead she sat and watched as Becky glugged the wine and gyrated to the music and the sound of the storm, which had become more intense so now it seemed to be above their heads.

"I think we need to get going," Clare said, "The football will start in ten minutes."

"Oh screw the football, screw them all," shrieked Becky, taking another swig of the wine. She refilled her glass and continued dancing, allowing the wine to spill as she moved. There was sweat on her brow. "This is much more.."

A clap of thunder obliterated her final word and the music stopped.

"Oh fuck," she said. " A bloody power cut. Where's the trip switch?"

Clare had noticed it at the top of the stairs. She told Becky and watched as she skipped across the terrace and went inside. The stairs were wooden, narrow and steep. Clare followed her up them. The electricity box was at the top on the landing. Becky tried to reach it but it was just too high.

"Bugger, I need something to stand on," she complained, looking around.

Joel's toy fire engine lay near the top step. Becky shoved it over with her bare foot and stepped onto it to reach. Clare could see up under her dress. Becky was wearing no underwear. There was another clap of thunder and Becky cursed. She tiptoed on the toy to reach higher and it slipped from beneath her foot. As the toy rolled away she lost her hold. The alarm triggered and its blue lights began to flash. Becky was small and light and spun like a wheel. By the time Clare reached the bottom of the stairs she was lying in a skewed heap on the stone floor. Her eyes were open but blank. There was a deep gash in her forehead. Her legs were at odd angles and her skirt was raised above her waist. Clare looked down at the bare brown torso, to the places she felt certain Liam had ventured only hours before. She crouched down and felt Becky's neck for a pulse. Nothing.

She stood back up and listened. Silence. As soon as it had come, the storm had passed. The pressure had risen and there a cool breeze replaced the previously thick air. Clare went back upstairs and walked into Becky and Mark's bedroom. She looked at herself in the dressing table mirror. Her face looked as pale as Liam's had earlier, beneath her emerging tan. Becky's red lipstick lay open on the table. She applied some carefully to her lips then she picked up her mobile; there was still no signal. It was ten past eight. She went back down the creaking stairs, stepped over Becky and left the house. I wonder who's winning, she contemplated as she made her way to the bar.

Anon *Walton on Thames*

"You're a risk taker,"
my lover says.
"No I'm not," I say. I smile at
him, "My husband's at work.
Finn's out and the big black
dog can't talk."
"Oh I wouldn't say that," he
says, looking at the big black
dog who is now standing at
the bedroom door, "Look at
him. Look how accusingly he
is staring at me."

Lucy Cavendish

Anon Walton on Thames
Lucy Cavendish

The big black dog is lying on the rug next to my bed. His eyes are closed and twitching sometimes. He looks as if he is chasing rabbits in his sleep but it's not convincing. He's just pretending because he can't stand the sight of my lover stretched out naked on my bed. It is ten o'clock in the morning. I am wearing stockings, a G-string, a black lace bra, high heels, make up, perfume. My hair is tousled, lipstick stained across my mouth, mascara smudged. I look in the mirror that reflects the bed and the sleeping dog next to it. Minutes ago I was looking at my lover as he hovered over me, turning me over and around and blowing on the back of my neck. I like to watch him as he kisses and caresses. He bends towards my body as if he's about to drink me up. I like the way his fingers linger. I like watching him when he closes his eyes. I am voyeuristic even of myself.

I glance at the end of the bed where the big black dog lies, eyes open now, patiently waiting for us to finish. I don't know how he gets back in to the bedroom. I keep shutting the door on him and yet somehow he manages to push it open. I almost want to lock him out but I feel so mean. The big black dog follows me everywhere. He is not used to being denied access to me. I just know he wouldn't like it. He hasn't said anything so far but…every time my lover appears, the big black dog pads after us, up the stairs, in to the room. It's weird.

I mean, who on earth wants to see their dog looking at them when they are in bed with their lover?

The big black dog was in here, a year ago, when we first got together. He sat at the end of the bed as my lover kissed the ends of my fingertips then he looked at me with such reproach that I was convinced he actually knew what was going on. He stared at me with his large chocolate eyes and said, 'don't do this.' And for a second I stopped. I pulled away. Had the big black dog spoken to me? But then my lover parted my legs and I closed my eyes and it all seemed to be part of the one and whole thing, the words of the big black dog and the tinged guilt of what my lover was doing with his tongue.

I hear the telephone ring. The dog's ears prick up.

"The telephone's ringing," he says. He looks at me in the mirror. I ignore him.

"Don't answer it," my lover says, pulling me back towards him. I hear the big black dog shift his weight from one side of his body to the other. The floorboards creak. It's an old house. The sound makes my lover jump.

"What's that?" he says nervously.

"The dog," I say. The phone is still ringing.

"The telephone's still ringing," says the dog, more insistently.

"I have to answer this," I say, "It might be the drama school."

My lover sighs.

"Fuck the school."

"No, Finn said he was feeling ill this morning. I told them to call if there was a problem. It's a Sunday. I made him go because...because."

We both know why. My husband is, uncharacteristically, away for the weekend. It is a chance. Our only chance. I get up and run downstairs to take the call. The big black dog pads after me. I pick up the receiver. He cocks his head to one side.

"I bet it's Finn," I tell him, "I bet he's ill. Don't you think? Poor Finn."
The big black dog casts his eyes downwards.

"Yes, poor Finn," he says.

"What?" I say.
The big black dog looks at me. His eyes are impenetrable.

"I'm going mad," I say.

"Mrs Scott?" says the voice at the end of the line.

"Yes it's me." I look away from the dog.

"It's the drama school. I'm afraid your son is…"

"I know," I say. "I'll be right there."
I run back up the stairs. For a second I imagine turning up to the office of Stagecoach in a lacy top and suspenders and it makes me smile, then I remember who I am. A married mother with a young child. Married women who have children do not wear *Agent Provocateur* and have three orgasms with a man who is not her husband before coffee break. I go back upstairs. My lover is still lying naked on my bed.

"Your mobile went," he says.
I look at the number flashing up on the screen.

"My husband," I say.
He raises his eyebrows. I get back on the bed and kiss him on the mouth. I notice the big black dog is standing at the bedroom door.

"For God's sake," I say to him, suddenly cross. "Can't you leave me alone for a minute?"
The big black dog turns his back on me.

"Suit yourself," he says and slopes off.

"You're a risk taker," my lover says.

"No I'm not," I say. I smile at him. "My husband's at work. Finn's out and the big black dog can't talk."

"Oh I wouldn't say that," he says, looking at the big black dog that is now standing at the bedroom door. "Look at him. Look how accusingly he is staring at me." I laugh.

"No, it's true," he says. "Just look at him. He's bristling with rage."

I glance at the big black dog. For a second I see he does seem angry but then he looks at me and his gaze softens.

"Are you alright?" I ask him.

"Yes," says the big black dog turning away.

"Did he just speak?" I ask.

My lover looks at me as if I have gone totally mad.

"God, you're talking to the dog," he says.

Four hours earlier.

I cannot tell you what a rush it was. He hadn't told me what day we were meeting. Usually we wait for a Monday lunchtime. That's when my phone starts bleeping. We never usually contact each other at the weekends. I used to think we might. I used to think he was so smitten with me that he'd have to contact me whenever, wherever. I thought he'd ring me, text me, ring me some more. I thought he'd crave me, never want to be away from me. Sometimes I think that's all I want, someone to need me and want me and spend time with me. In a way, I thought the sex would be secondary. But no. Our meetings are all about sex and when he is not with me or in me, my lover seems to be the epitome of self-control. I hear nothing from him. It's as if he has died. And yet he texts me all the time during the week. I can be in the shops, the gym, wherever and it sounds as if I have a small bomb waiting to go off in my pocket. He texts me explicit things, what he would like to do to me, where he'd like to do it and with what. I get them all the time and they make me blush as I walk the big black dog round the fields. But, at the weekends, my lover ceases to exist. Weekends, he explained to me once, is not the time for us. Only this one. Only this once.

Weekends are for family walks with the big black dog. The big black dog likes family walks. They make him happy. I know this because sometimes he looks so joyous, he almost smiles. He says thank you when he sees me get his lead and the bag of bread for the ducks and put on Finn's Wellingtons. The big black dog shakes his head and wags his tail back and forth and back and forth in excited expectation and sometimes his tail hits Finn and Finn wails loudly and then the big black dog looks guilty and sad.

The rest of the time his tongue hangs out and when he runs fast his saliva drips down his mouth and on to his chest. I play make believe games on these walks. I pretend that I am happy. I rise above myself and see us – me, my husband, our son, the dog and I think 'look at that contented little family, how jolly they all are' and then that makes me feel good because it means I am acting my part so well.

Sometimes I get really in to it. I hold my husband's hand and we look at the ducks and we talk about Finn. We feed swans bread and then run away from them because, when you have a plastic bag, swans tend to chase you because they bloody well know you have bread and they're greedy things really. The big black dog hates the swans. If they come on to the bank near us he barks at them and they hiss back and make their wings flap majestically swirling the air around. Finn cries when he sees this. He tells me he thinks the swans will break the big black dog but it never happens.

What the big black dog likes most is to swim. He finds a stick and he leaps up and down and up and down until one of us throws it in to the water for him. Then he dives in. He literally hurls himself from the bank and drops in a flurry of black fur in to the river. Then he sets out, paddling to the stick, snorting as the water gets up his nose. Then he ploughs on back to us, stick in mouth, tail wagging like an out-of-control rudder and he hauls himself up on the bank and shakes madly and we all squeal and run away from him and it makes him laugh.

When we get back in to the car, the big black dog sinks down in to the footwell and gently steams in the heat of the radiator and soon he smells like an old mop. I turn and pat him on the head and he licks my hand gratefully.

"Thank you," he says.

I see myself in the rear view mirror. Do I look as if I am losing my mind?

Two days ago, though, everything was different. I just didn't know it was going to be different. I was lying in bed half-awake, half-asleep, my husband's back towards me, about to get up and leave on his trip, the big black dog lying by the side of the bed. I was gazing at the hairs on his back which form a ridge of curls when the rest of the hair on his flanks are as straight as tiny arrows when my phone bleeped. It was so quiet and there it was BLEEP BLEEP and the big black dog raised his hackles.

"Oh God," he said, "It's him isn't it?"

I put a hand down to him.

"Sshh," I said and I stroked him a bit. His body felt tense under his fur.

I knew it was him and I couldn't understand why he was texting me at the time. My hand shot out as if I had been given an electric shock and I grabbed the phone. My husband gave a faint snore. I breathed out carefully, long and slow. I hid the telephone under the covers and read.

"We have to meet this morning. It's important."

I looked at my husband. He still hadn't stirred. I jabbed at the letters of the phone.

"What time?" I didn't put a kiss on the end. It was too early in the morning for that. And, anyway, he hadn't put a kiss on the end of his message. That much I really had noticed.

I got up. The big black dog looked at me warily.

"Walk?" I said to him.

He jumped up, wagging his tail.

"Oh yes please," he said.

It was while we were walking up the hill and the big black dog was bounding along in front of me, that I felt it. Something was going to change. I just knew it was. The thought of it hit me as I watched the big black dog's tail streaming out behind him. This is all going to change, I thought, and there's nothing I can do to stop it. It's important. That's what he said. What could be so important?

Sometimes you can't stop fate. That's the problem isn't it? We all go along in a state of near oblivion, never aware of the hand of fate waving at us above our heads but sometimes, just sometimes, you get an inkling, a pre-warning, a sense that something isn't quite right. I was on an aeroplane coming back from the States with a man I'd just spent a week with. We weren't lovers. Not in the true sense of the word. We'd kissed a bit and gone to Mexico just to see what it was like and then we'd come home again. I was much younger then, him older than me but he'd told me in the aeroplane on the way home that he couldn't see himself living to much more than 52.

"I'll come and see you before then," he said. How my friend would laugh if he saw me now but he can't and he didn't because he died of cancer a few years back, just before his 50th birthday.

Ten minutes later, I was walking towards the top of the hill. I stopped near the top to check the phone. No message back.

"Why does he want to meet today?" I asked the big black dog. He had stopped running up the hill now and was waiting for me at the stile. "What do you think he wants? Do you think he's going to split up with me?" The dog wagged his tail. "Oh stop being so happy about it. You've never liked him and I know why." I picked the big black dog's stick up. "You just want it to be fun and games don't you?" I said as he started bouncing around. "God, I wish I had your energy."

I looked down from the top of the hill. The sun was emerging from behind a long wisp of cloud. I got my phone out.

"What time do you want to meet?" I texted, then I sat and waited for a reply. The big black dog sat and looked out across the hill.

"Why isn't he replying?" I said.
The dog let out a long sigh.

"How am I supposed to know?" he said.
I walked on.
It was only when I had gone down the other side

my phone bleeped.

"9.30?"

"9.45." I replied.

This is what I do for my lover.

This is how I start. As the bath fills, I undress. I take off my early morning kit. I peel off the jeans, the T-shirt, the jumper, the fleecy socks, the big knickers. I lower myself in to the bath. I bathe in warm, soapy, bubbly water. I know what he likes. He likes me cleaned, perfumed, smooth. I soap myself under my arms, around my breasts, everywhere. Then I find my razor and gently de-stubble myself. I make my legs hairless like silk. My under arms are denuded of everything. I add scented oils to the bath to soften my skin. Then I get out. As I dry I lay out the clothes. I start from the skin outwards. Some days I wear something simple – a pretty bra, matching frilly knickers, hold-ups. Today though, I decide on G-string and suspenders. I moisturise my skin. I dab perfume on my wrists, my neck, my breast bone. When I'm ready, I start to dress. I bend this way and that in order to fasten the hooks on my bra. I snap on the suspenders. I contort myself to see what I look like in the mirror. Then I put on high black stilettos and stand in front of the mirror to put my make up on. The bathroom door opens. I reach for my robe. It's the big black dog. He lies down on the carpet near my feet and looks up at me at me as I kohl the rims of my eyelids and add blusher to my cheeks.

"What do I look like?" I say. I do a small pirouette in front of the dog. "Don't answer," I say. I tie on the robe and go to open the back door.

"You shouldn't be doing this," the dog says from

behind me. "Think of your marriage, your child….you should stop taking this risk. I think I might run off with one of your stockings."

"Oh shut up," I say. "You'll ladder it anyway so don't."

"You're addictive," my lover says as he gets up and looks out of the window.

"You're naked and I have to go."
He laughs and lies back down.

"Lie with me," he says. "We never get to do this. We never get to spend…time together." He runs his hands down me, his skin on my skin. He kisses me gently on the lips. "You're lovely," he says, propping himself up, "But still…is this a risk worth taking?"
I look at him.

"Is that what you have come to say to me?" I ask. "Is this the urgency?" He looks at me. He shrugs.

"It's dangerous," he says. "Maybe too dangerous. I think that's what you like about this. You are a dangerous woman."

I want to tell him it's not too dangerous for me. I want to say that I need him, that I want him, that these brief moments of desiring him are not just about passion. They are about necessity. Anyway, I wouldn't have put him down as being someone who was scared of taking a risk. Maybe I am wrong.
The phone rings again.

"Finn's drama," I say. "I have to go."
He sighs. "There's something I want to say to you," he says.
I put my fingers over his lips.

"Not now," I say.

"I'll text you later," he says. "I am worried I…"

46

He looks towards the big black dog lying outside the bedroom door.

"God, it's as if that dog is judging everything we do. It's freaky."

I get up and walk down the stairs. The big black dog follows me.

"Where are we going?" he says.

"To the school," I say, "Finn's ill. Are you coming?"

The big black dog wags his tail, expectantly. He cocks his head to one side. He always looks so curious.

"Well, are you?" I say.

The big black dog whines.

"What is it?" I say to him. The big black dog stares at me. "You're staring," I said. "You're making me feel bad. Stop it."

The big black dog whines again.

"He's still upstairs," he says. "I'm not sure if you should leave him here by himself."

"I'm not in the mood for this," I tell the dog.

"Oh God," I say as I walk in to the kitchen to get the car keys. Something pierces my foot.

"Shit!" A needle of pain shoots up my leg. I sit down heavily on the sofa.

"What the…"

I bend to look at my foot. A small piece of pointed Lego has lodged itself in the padded bit between my toes.

The big black dog cocks his ears and whines again.

"Poor you," he says.

"Yes, I know," I say. "Poor me."

My lover puts his head around the door.

"You OK?" he says.

I nod.

"I'm off now. I'll text you."

"When?" I ask.

"Later, before the match. Will HE still be away?"
I raise my eyebrows. "Yes," I say.

"Oh, well make sure you tell me before then," I
say, a touch sarcastically.

He shifts from foot to foot.

"Oh just say it," I say. "Just say it."

"No," he says and then he closes the door.

"It's not good news is it?" I ask the big black dog.

"Probably not," says the dog. "How's your foot?"

"I've got to stop imagining that you are talking to
me," I say to the dog, "It's getting ridiculous."

The big black dog gives me a grin.

"I think you quite like it," he says.

Finn is sitting just inside the door of the drama school
when I get there.

"I'm ill Mummy," he says.

"I know darling," I say. I go and give him a big
hug. "Shall I take you home?"

Finn nods and sniffs a bit. I am aware of the fact that I
still have my black lacy push-up bra on under my white
shirt. I suddenly feel a bit conspicuous.

Finn clutches my hand as we walk to the car.

"What shall we do now?" he says.

"Go home," I say. "I thought you were ill."

"I am ill," he says, "But it's really a headache."

"Well," I say, "I have the dog in the car. Do you
want to take him for a walk? The fresh air might clear
your head."

Finn nods enthusiastically.

"Ooh yes," he says, "Do you have his lead?"

The dog wags his tail when he sees Finn. He leaps from

the boot of the car on to the back seat and licks him. Finn giggles.

"Are you alright?" the dog asks him. "Is he alright?" he asks me.

"Yes," I say, "He's fine and now we are going to take you for a walk."

The dog smiles at me.

"Thank you," he says.

"That's alright," I say. "It'll do us all good."

"Mum," says Finn, he gives me a quizzical look, "Can dogs talk?"

I laugh. "Of course not," I say.

"But I think he can talk."

"Do you?" I say. "Well, he has such an expressive face you probably just think he can talk."

"No Mum. He really can. He tells me things but I am never sure if they are true because, when he sees things, he sees them with his doggy eyes doesn't he and they're not like our eyes are they?"

"No," I say, driving away from town, "Dogs actually do see things differently. I think everything is black and white to them, something like that."

"But Mrs Smith told me animals can't talk."

"Why were you even talking about it?"

"Because," whispers Finn, looking furtively around him, "I think animals can talk and I told my teacher Mrs Smith they can." He looks at the big black dog. "He can talk mummy, can't he?"

I look at the big black dog. The big black dog avoids my gaze.

"He tells me stories," Finn continues. "Sometimes at night, when I can't sleep, he tells me all sorts of things."

"Like what?" I say, staring at the dog but trying to keep my voice light.

"Oh all sorts of things," says Finn happily. "Like he told me yesterday what Mrs Rose's cat gets up to in the day time when Mrs Rose is out."

"Did he?" I say.

"Yes. That cat does terrible things. He caught a robin the other day and he tortured it for an hour at least. That's what the big black dog said so when I saw Mrs Rose's cat later on in the afternoon, I squirted it with the hose pipe."

"Oh," I say, looking at the big black dog. The big black dog stares out of the window.

"What else does he tell you?"

"He tells me you like having a bath when I am at school. He says you put lovely smelling things in it."

"Does he?" The big black dog shifts imperceptibly on the seat.

"And he says you have beautiful things you like to wear and…"

"Time to go," I say suddenly. I start the car up.

"Where are we going mummy?" says Finn.

"To the river," I say.

When we get there, I put the lead on the big black dog.

"Why are you doing that Mummy?" says Finn. "You know how much he likes running around."

"Yes, I do," I say. "But I'm worried about the swans. There are cygnets here and swans get very protective of their young. They might try to hurt the dog or even kill it." I tighten the lead around my hand. "And we don't want that do we?"

Finn shakes his head slowly and then turns to look at the ducks.

50

"No we don't want that do we?" I say to the dog again.

The dog doesn't say anything. I look at my phone. No message.

It is the evening now and my husband is standing in the kitchen surveying some pots. He has come home early. He says he missed me, missed Finn. I am feeling jittery so I am drinking a glass of wine. The big black dog is in his bed. He is staring at me but I don't care. I am feeling reckless. I am feeling abandoned. There has been no message. My phone hasn't bleeped once. He can't even be bothered to tell me it is over. I want to talk to the big black dog about it but since I put him on the lead, he is refusing to talk to me. He didn't even thank me for his walk which is highly unusual.

"What are you doing?" I ask my husband.

"I'm making dinner," my husband says, "I can catch the second half."

"Oh, yes the World Cup final," I say.
My husband gives me a quizzical look. "How do you know that? You hate football."

"What are you making?" I say, ignoring his question..

"Pasta." He motions towards the cooker where a pot is bubbling away.

"Right," I say.

"With pesto," he says. "It's quick."
Neither of us blink.

"Is there anything up with the dog?" he asks me.
"He seems a bit low."

"Have you asked him?"
My husband laughs.

"Oh yeah, I did ask him and he said it's because

51

England aren't in the final I mean…"
Suddenly, I hear a phone bleeping. I know it's mine.
Christ! My husband stares at me.

"It's your phone," he says as the big black dog
leaves the room.

"I know," I say lightly. I go over to him and look
inside the pan. "Maybe the pasta is ready."

"No," my husband says, "It's only been in a
minute."

"Oh," I say. My phone bleeps again.

"Why don't you check your messages?" my
husband asks, "The phone's in your bag isn't it?"

"My bag's in the hall. It won't be important. I'll
check later."
Suddenly the big black dog appears. He is carrying my
phone in his mouth. He looks at me. I look at him.

"No," I say, "Please don't." The phone bleeps
again, muffled now by the dog's fleshy gums. He looks at
me once more, raises an eyebrow, then walks over to my
husband and drops the phone at his feet.

"Oh my God," I say, "Why have you done that?"

"You know why," says the big black dog. "I told
you it would bring nothing but pain. I love you and it has
to stop and now it will."

"You're talking to the dog," my husband says as
he bends to pick up the phone, "You've lost your mind.
You do know that don't you?"

He opens the message and then just looks at me,
his mouth open, face pale, fists clenched.

"Oh my God," he says, "Who is this from? It
says, it says…Oh God, Oh God. No. I don't believe it. I
don't believe you'd let someone do that to you…what the
fuck is going on?" What the fuck? He says the thing he

wanted to tell you is he wants to fuck you up the..Jesus!"
I just stand there and stare at him.

"That's torn it," says the big black dog happily
as my husband comes towards me, face contorted, fists
clenched harder, "But don't worry. I'll bite him if it all
gets too awful. That's a good idea, don't you think?"

Mrs Blythe *Knebworth*

*"The music was open
two pages from the molto
allargando – tonight
they would work on the
ending... Just then, the wildest
notion entered her head. She
might just have a little glass of
wine before he arrived."*

Rachel Jackson

really needs to, um, tease the listener."

"You're my listener. You would rather be teased, then?"

She coloured and lowered her eyes to middle C until his bark of a laugh released her.

"Just try it, please,"

"I'll give it a go."

He played the notes almost as she had. She stopped short of applause.

"Good!"

"Pretty sexy isn't it?" he laughed.

Yes, she wanted to say, it's Mae goddamn West, but she simply smiled and turned the page.

He stared at the fresh bars, looked at her as if she'd made a joke and turned the page back. "Sorry, do you mind? Just think I'd better do it again, for luck."

"Ok, go ahead."

The hour had gone downhill from there - or rather she had. She watched his hands closely, but forgot to note the fingering. When he'd loudly fumbled some chords and turned to her for help, he caught her staring at the back of his head with an unforgivable expression. For the first time she did not take to the keyboard herself, advising him instead over his shoulder. She did not trust her hands; wrong notes would just be too, too exposing. For the first time, when he rose to leave at nine o'clock, she felt she had done a bad job.

By the next afternoon Mrs. Blythe still felt skittish, in need of an anchor. Franz eyed her from his corner, whiskers twitching, crouching fat and suspicious. This would not do at all. It was high time to revisit Bach. She lifted the piano stool and found him on top of the pile, Goldberg variations waiting. To play a solid, G major theme and then work through its many delicate stages of evolution was always such a balm, such a calming process. Now more than ever she desired his pedantic brilliance, that mathematician's soul. It looked simple on the page, this complex interweaving, but her fingers would remember their role, as they always did. That was part of the magic, the remembering. She loved to see it happen in others; what other reason was there to teach?

Her fingers poised over the starting notes, wrists correctly raised…but her hands refused to ease their tension and just a few bars in she found that she was no longer willing to chase down the notes with metronomic precision. An idea had occurred, one that made Bach's company seem unusually tedious. She smoothed her skirt, rose to put Johann back in his place and left the room.

The computer was still humming in the corner of the hall. She launched the internet and clicked until the music started to pour out, the thrill of that trill, the euphoric glissando. Her lips set themselves into a kind of determination and she turned up the volume as high as it would go.

She hurried to her bedroom, leaving the door wide open to let the first passage of sleazy abandon blare in. She undressed and folded her clothes on to the chair, not wanting to miss the part where the main theme burst through once more.

Pulling on her slip, trying not to see her husband's grip upon its silk, she eased herself under the lilac duvet. Her glasses were placed on the bedside table. She closed her eyes and let her hand settle upon her stomach. The agitated notes played themselves out through her fingertips, delving right inside the music. Should she? Such a long time ago... the decision overtook her and she parted her feet towards the far corners of the bed, letting her fingers run a scale over her abdomen, then lower. Here came the theme, there he was again, with a confidence that bordered on swagger. Her touch became quite unlike herself: foreign, jaunty. The warmth built inside her, rising, as if in tiny bubbles, to the surface of her skin. Too soon, the pianist was inside the moment with her, frighteningly wild, at the point where the notes flew off the stave and the American willed both player and listener to take leave of all but one of their senses, just for fun. She too was all in the moment, seeing nothing behind her eyelids but silver and scarlet, becoming pure mind and sound and dancing fingers. It would not last, so she hurried a little, urging herself on, seizing each bar as a chance to create greater tension. Her breath came fast and shallow as she perfectly conquered each note, at last. Brillante, the score dictated, brillante, brillante, sparkling... And then there was a softening, a falling, a tumbling back down to earth.

After some minutes, her eyes opened onto an expanse of white. The Artex ceiling. How could interior décor be used as a form of torture? Angus had given her the idiot-look when she had commented on it as the gawky estate agent had showed them around. Perfectly serviceable. It apparently mattered not one jot that she could feel it pressing on her whenever they got into bed, especially on those nights when she had cause to stare at the ceiling for longer than usual. You would have thought he would have paid someone, done something, in the nine intervening years, but no. A waste of money, apparently. A taboo subject. Not a decisive man, her husband. Not like a lawyer.

There was no Artex in the Hatfield flat that they had invested in so that he could stay over when lectures kept him on campus until late in the evening. It was convenient. He would spend the odd night at the flat, and then more and more, until somehow the nights at home became the odd ones and she became the convenience. She had, quite rightly, addressed the situation, as any normal wife would.

"Couldn't you just, you know, spend more time here again," she had asked, straining to hear. It had sounded like he was in a café. A pause, a clatter of china.

"I think I'd rather not."

Just like that. Nothing personal, a simple matter of preference. Her husband had left her because the alternative didn't take his fancy quite as much. The ballast of their life together had been unimaginably eroded by - what? Too much time passing over it? – until it was so light that he had simply drifted off, floated away...

Suddenly she felt ravenous. She went to the kitchen and stood at the fridge, still in her cream slip. She absent-mindedly pulled out a thin slice of Parma ham and draped it into her mouth. Such sluttish behaviour was precisely the problem. Every time she let her mind drift into the lazy, longing fantasies, she ended up far from where she should be, stranded on some lush, wild shore where eating cold, foreign meats with your fingers would be a daily occurrence. Even now, sated and calm, she imagined. Possibilities coming at her every which way, all with Martin as the central theme. Too weak to resist, she let her mind roam over the most outlandish idea of them all, that of absolute happiness waiting just around the corner. She did not see them running, hands joined, through cornfields or on some balmy beach. They were too old and unlikely for all that. She did not picture them at all, instead she simply heard those few bars he had last attempted, the most outrageously sentimental passage, the love story. When she first put on the CD she simply had thought the phrases to be perfectly designed to manipulate the emotions, almost comical, somewhat vulgar, but relatively simple to play. Right now, as they danced in her mind, she didn't really think at all, simply felt them to be quite innocently beautiful. So much possibility…

This was absurd. He might be pushing fifty but he was a pupil and he had come to her in good faith. She was simply not qualified, either in life or in Gershwin. She would have to pass Martin on to another teacher, this was madness. But no, she couldn't. Could she? She could. She would tell him this was to be their last lesson, that she was referring him on to someone who was completely qualified, better for him. More professional… although, no. She wouldn't put it quite like that. More accomplished, maybe. He might not mind.

It was a surprise to her, then, that at about half past seven the following Sunday night she found herself slipping on entirely the wrong sort of shoes. A good three inches high, the colour of mulled wine. Quite impossible to get the feel of the pedals in them, should she choose to take to the stool. She had already – a good hour before - dabbed on a thin layer of foundation, properly, with a sponge, and lightly traced her eyes in black. A smattering of mascara, then that was enough. Nothing too devastating. The shoes were a compelling afterthought. Quite irresistible.

The music was open two pages from the molto allargando – tonight they would work on the ending. Her feet tapped on the wooden floor. Angus had never quite come round to the exposed floorboards but she had insisted – carpets ate up all the sound. Just then, the wildest notion entered her head. She might just have a little glass of wine before Martin arrived. It was a bad idea, it would ruin her playing, but perhaps she might just sit and watch him tonight, merely encourage and advise. In any case she couldn't play properly in these shoes. She might, even, set out a pair of glasses and the bottle on this side table so that afterwards, if he wanted they could talk a little about the piece and anything else that arose…

Franz followed her to the kitchen, mewling insistently in a way that jangled her nerves. She grabbed a bottle of Syrah, the glasses and some dry food then clipped over to his feeding mat next to her piano and threw a handful of the latter into his bowl. A third of it spattered out of the bowl and bounced on the oak. Her irritation rose, he'd already had his supper, the greedy little tyke, no wonder he was getting porky.

She set the metronome ticking to calm herself down. Funny habit, one that only started at around the time that Angus had stopped phoning. It sounded just like the beating heart of a particularly frigid man. Never raced, never faltered. Meanwhile, the clock above the piano was silent but equally reliable: 8.05pm. She listened to the tick-tick for a full minute and all she could think about was the unavoidable fact that he was not there. He had not come. If he did not come back, as well he might not, then something irreplaceable would have been broken, beyond the immediate disaster

68

of his absence. He was, after all, the man who came back. It was there in his solid hands, translated into that eagerness and that tireless repetition of the more difficult phrases. There was something about it, the way he entered one's head like a familiar but forgotten tune that made her believe in the absolute rightness of him. Yet he was not here. She could see now that she had set too much store by it. But of course he was not here: tonight was the World Cup final. It must have kicked off long ago and he must have forgotten to cancel. Men loved their sport, didn't they? He was probably with friends, unaware that she was waiting, cool drink in his hand. Simply too shaming. It was not just that she had practised the final two pages over and over, or rehearsed witty comments about certain evocative phrases. It was that she suddenly saw the terrible foolishness of it all, every secret thought, all that unwanted desire.

Foolish in her high-heeled shoes, unwanted in her lipstick and smooth foundation. She was an instructor, no more, one who had crossed the line. Unforgivable. But she didn't ask forgiveness, just that someone help her stem this rising tide of embarrassment pushing higher in her chest. As she watched the ticking box, her eyes began to sting. A rush of noise swept the street as some new outrage was committed on the pitch. Every window was open, every TV on save her own. No Martin, no wonder. Embarrassment started to feel like panic. All the weeks of waiting and practising and longing when she should just have been focusing on the Rhapsody. Foolish, unwanted. He was not coming back: it was already ten past eight. Slowly her breath began to keep time too, a slow two-four, catching, choking back each sob.

Eyes wet, deafened, she sensed him before she

saw him. He stumbled through the doorway, too big, too fast, indigo book in hand. His sudden presence hit her like a wall of sound.

"I'm so sorry, Emily."

He pressed her name firmly into the air, a starting note. It was not until she heard her name in his mouth that she realised how important it was that she hear it. Something tightened, just where her neck met her chest. He was there, so very full of himself, in the truest sense. No swaggering at all, simply back again. She did not try to wrestle back the wave of joy that crushed her. She knew, now, what this meant.

He stared at her as he moved towards the stool, smiling less than usual. In one glance he took in the wine, the shoes, the lipstick, the spilled cat biscuits. He noted the two glasses. He did not ask why her hand brushed at her cheeks, did not mention the football. He just sat, did not smile and awaited instruction.

She took a slow, silent breath and then commanded, "Let's go back to the beginning shall we?"

And then she waited to hear that startling sweep of notes.

by altering one factor. Not everything is as it seems, she tells herself. Change can happen, if you alter one tiny element.

She tells herself so about herself too. Because she knows if people were to look at her from the outside they might think one thing, whereas inside it is possible to be completely different. She doesn't like the way people are so quick to judge by appearances. She's been guilty of it herself, of course; snap decisions based on surfaces. But now she is older, heading towards her later twenties, she understands exteriors and interiors are not always the same thing. On the outside Ella may appear fat and unhappy, but inside she is carrying her lighter, happier self, the one she hopes will appear for the world soon, when she has finally lost some weight. She even has a name for her alter-ego: Lela. She was pleased when she chose the anagram of her own name. It felt honest: just a reordering of herself, which might be all it would take to change her from Ella, the heavy, single woman whose thighs stick to her chair when she's typing, to Lela, the nimble girl who wears skinny jeans and has a belly button ring.

Ella has a very detailed understanding of Lela, how she looks, how she dresses. Lela often wears skinny jeans, figure-hugging but practical. She's a practical girl, in fact, though she's definitely feminine. She's curvaceous, not anaemic like some of the supermodels. More Angelina than Kate. She does like to show her midriff. Sometimes Ella thinks it's a bit immature, but then, its flat tone and the belly button ring justify it. And Lela's got lovely dusky brown skin. She wears colours that set her skin tone off – often orange, which is a particularly difficult colour to carry, Ella knows, but somehow Lela always looks good in it, her long black curly hair swept up into a ponytail. According to the name site she checked, Lela means "dark haired beauty". Her name suits her.

Ella has hand-drawn quite a few pictures of Lela, just to get a sense of how she might look in different outfits. Having those picture blu-tacked to the wall made it easier to get a reasonable likeness of her onscreen. It had taken Ella a number of long sessions to perfect Lela's image on The Game. Thankfully she'd had a few practice runs at creating other avatars. They had been more experimental, not projections of reality. Lela has the same birth date as Ella, the same eye colour. There have been nips and tucks, of course, but fundamentally, they're the same woman. Chiselled from the same lump of rock, you might say. It's just, Ella tells herself, that to get to Lela, you have to chisel a bit deeper into the lump of rock, smooth the stone more, refine the sculpture. That's what everyone does online, airbrush out the blemishes you'd see if you were in the real world. Here, in The Game, you can leave behind the imperfections.

When Ella had first joined The Game, it had been because she wanted to play. But she's withdrawn from the competitive element. Now it's more social. One of the nice things is that it's on 24 hours a day. Of course, you tend to socialise in specific time zones, make most of your friends in that place. That is if you want to have immediate responses. But Lela's the sort of person who likes to think about her interaction sometimes. She is agile, but considered, doesn't want to rush into things too much. That's the appeal really: you can play it at your own speed. The Game recognises that social speeds vary. Sometimes you want to layer, get deep; at others you want to short-hand, get to the point quickly.

Lela's profile outlines her interests. She's signed up to a couple of activities; rock-climbing, orienteering. That's her energetic, physical side. But she likes to chat too and has recently joined a couple of chat rooms: music radio discussion groups and one called "just chilling". It's a place to meet people, whoever turns up. It reminds Lela of the bar scenes in Star Wars where all sorts of extraterrestrials hang out together. In The Game most of them aren't aliens, but some avatars do have extreme features. Some of the guys have tails, or horns, and then, of course, there are always the ones who are ridiculously well-endowed. Lela tends to avoid those guys, the ones who are blatantly out to pull.

But recently Lela's been feeling the need to connect emotionally. Life can't be completely about creating a home and interior décor. Her home is pretty complete now: it's fairly minimalist, quite white and Zen with some stylish 20th century flourishes, Egg chairs, chrome fittings, moving artwork on the walls, which are circular and which slide open on command. It allows for open-plan living in a completely different way, vertical as well as horizontal. Lela's whole ceiling slides to one side so she can view the night sky lying on her sofa. The outside courtyard is quite Zen too: lots of concentric circles of stones. It all fits in with Lela's interest in the Orient. She knows a bit about Eastern philosophy and thought, but wants to know more, which is why she enters the Yin and Yang area.

It's a very balanced part of The Game, which you'd expect, quite monochrome, but with gold angles, like you'd see on Thai temples. It's a place to meditate or just chat, away from the frantic pace of ordinary life. It's here Lela meets Fin.

- Like the shark, though I have Celtic blood. You?

- A mixture. Think I'm a global citizen, but fascinated by the East. That's why I'm here, in Yin and Yang.

- Not been here before, but like the vibe. It's good to get out of the comp zones sometimes. I've been working up a bit of a sweat over there.

Fin is very tall and blonde. He has tattoos all over his torso. There's a snake meandering across his chest, its tail morphing into a twist of thorns that circle his biceps, intricate black text entwining his throat.

- What's the neck design?

- Part of the Baghavad Gita. Hindu religious text. It means "The wise see knowledge and action as one."

- It's beautiful.

Ella, zooms in, Lela's hand gently touching his neck.

- It's Sanskrit font.

- The word "avatar" comes from Sanskrit. Means "incarnation"- if you believe Wikipedia.

They chat back and forth, swapping information about Eastern mythology, Buddhism. Different forms of yoga.

- We should go together, check out those temples.

- Great. Let's make a plan. Tomorrow, same time?

Which is how it all started. Lela has a date in Yin and Yang to plan an adventure to another country. A research trip, some might call it a holiday. That's one of the things to be negotiated with Fin. Whether they're going to go alone, or take others with them. People often travel in groups in The Game, but their conversation had just been between the two of them. He'd flipped it into private mode at some point. Ella couldn't remember where, though she could have tracked it onscreen if she'd wanted. It didn't matter. Fin had wanted to keep their discussion exclusive. He was interested enough just in her to spend a good half an hour chatting with her alone, and yet he hadn't abused the moment.

Ella appreciated his sensitivity. He obviously shared her interest in philosophy and spirituality too. She spent the next two hours researching destinations inside The Game, and on the web. She wanted to impress him and keep him interested. It was gone four by the time she turned the computer off, wolfed a bag of pretzels, drank some milk and lay down on the bed fully-clothed, too tired to undress. She watched the grey dawn seep over Perivale.

And so, as with many relationships, it begins with a chance encounter. It deepens, that exchange of information, half-banter, feigned ignorances, teasings. Lela and Fin are becoming an item, a pairing in a virtual world of electronic pulses and lit screens. And, one step removed, Ella feeds the romance, obsessing over it the way one does with a new relationship. What should Lela wear? How to keep him interested. It doesn't interfere too much with the rest of her life: the rest of her life is here, anyway, in these rooms. Ella doesn't have to go out to work – the documents are emailed to her, and she can proofread them at the desk and phone in any amendments. They're quite happy if she just emails corrected texts back, which means she can work whatever hours she wants. It brings her enough money. It's paid straight into her bank account. Everything electronically transferred. She doesn't need to see people and they don't need to see her.

She can do so much online now, she doesn't

need to go out. In fact, she doesn't, hasn't been for three years. It crept up gradually on her. For a while she'd make the effort, but her panic attacks became more acute. One time she really thought she was going to have a heart attack. There was a distinct constriction across her chest, like someone was tightening metal rope or hawsers around her. She couldn't breathe, but at the same time she felt her heart pumping in panic. Blood rushed through her ears like the sound of waves receding on pebbled beaches. She'd managed to get home but had been violently sick, kneeling on the bathroom floor, holding on to the toilet as if it was an anchor. Maybe it had been a mild ear infection, but somehow she'd never quite managed to get herself outside since. There wasn't any need anyway. Tesco delivers. Rabindha, an old friend from college who lives around the corner drops by once or twice a fortnight and brings her anything she needs. The flat is warm and safe and dry. And she can hook up with her friends, see Fin, any time she likes. Doesn't even have to get dressed, she tells herself, though she is aware of her body more since they met, and she's been taking a bit more care. Maybe she showers slightly more, washes her hair, dries her body a bit more carefully, dusting the crevices with talcum powder. There aren't any mirrors in the flat big enough to see more than her face in. She doesn't regard herself, doesn't have a whole picture of her own body. It's not something she wants to think about, but maybe there is an incremental physical awareness of her own self. Sometimes Rabindha will come over and they'll indulge in a bit of pampering: she'll give Rabindha a manicure in exchange for having her eyebrows threaded.

Fin asks about perfume. She tells him she doesn't

wear one in particular, though she likes the smell of jasmine. The question circulates inside her, and one evening whilst she's waiting to meet with him again in Yin and Yang, she finds herself imagining his scent. Metallic somehow, like coins held tightly in a damp palm, with something sharp, slightly edgy, citrus possibly. Thinking it, she feels warm and energised.

Ella isn't a virgin. She slept with a couple of blokes at college. One was just a guy she met at a gig. A one night stand. But Robin had been more serious and she'd enjoyed the sex more. Neither of them was particularly adventurous, it was what you might describe as straightforward, but she'd enjoyed it. She had found pleasure in the touching and being held, and they had been close for a while. Then things got complicated. When her mum had got sick, he'd not been up to the task and he'd sort of melted away and left her. There hadn't been an official end to things, he'd just turn up less and less. He'd appear unannounced at her flat, they'd watch a bit of telly, have sex and then he'd leave, mumbling something about classes, essay deadlines. It was infrequent, irregular. Then one day, she noticed he hadn't been for a fortnight. She tried his mobile and he didn't answer. She wasn't going out much by then anyway, she felt bad about herself, she was eating too much. She burrowed inside.

- I love the scent of jasmine, Fin is in Yin and Yang. He kisses her neck.
- I've missed you.
- Ditto.
- Tell me about your day.
- No, just more kisses.

He puts an arm around her in response.

Ella's left hand drops to her thigh, her right still typing, and slips under her dressing gown, between her thighs. She squeezes them tightly together, her fingertips sliding between and touches herself in a way she hasn't for many months.

- Nice? Fin asks.

She rocks gently backwards and forwards on his suggestions, wet, warm, tight. It only takes a few seconds for her to be released, her mind disengaging briefly, and tense pleasure pulsating outwards from this one point, like a pebble dropped in water, diffusing through her whole body. She hears her own breathing, her skin is clammy, a trace of sweat on her upper lip.

- You good, Lela?
- Yes, just had a white-out.
- Me too.
- Good. I'm pleased.
- Feels good. Good to connect.
- Agree. Meeting you, Fin has been very special. I'm not good with words, but I want you to know that.
- Ditto. Special. Not many like you, Lela.

He kisses her again, strokes her shoulders.

- Gottago, Sweet. Sorry tonight was brief. More Yin and Yang tmrw @ 8?

She agrees and smiles to herself. Is "Yin and Yang" now their own private language for what just happened? He calls her Sweet, has his own pet name for her.

Ella closes The Game down and lies on the sofa, her dressing gown falling open, she regards her breasts in the blue computer light. She imagines Fin doing the same, stroking them gently, holding their fullness in his hands. He thinks she's special. The car headlights sweep in waves across her ceiling, defining and redefining the shadows of the blinds, but failing to illuminate the woman on the sofa, her back arched, hand guiding her lover's between her spread-eagled thighs.

She will lie here all night entwined with him, falling in love. That's what it is, isn't it? Some reawakening of the need for another, a connection that repositions you in relation to someone else, and yourself. It is pulling Ella out from her cocoon, unfurling her. But the metamorphosis requires something else. Perhaps something that will emerge the following evening, when the dual-carriageway is at its quietest. Now the cars are shifting quite readily, their lights traversing the dull tarmac, and arcing over her ceiling. West London is grey and unenticing. Ella hardly regards it, centred on her rendezvous with Fin. She's going to give him some poetry. She's dug out The Prophet, thinks he'll like the meditations on pleasure and love.

She logs on to The Game on the dot of eight. He's already there waiting for her. There's a nervousness in both of them this evening, as if their exchanges have changed in tempo. He looks different somehow.

- I want to take you somewhere, out of Yin and Yang. For a while. Though wanna comebaclater. She relinquishes control of Lela. He portals them both to Asia. They're on a beach, the sky pink and orange, the sea a rippling mirror, dolphins silhouetted in brief arcs above its surface.

- I've never brought anyone here before.
- It's beautiful. Really.
- My design. Fin's private paradise.
- Like the waterfall. A rainbow cascade tumbles off a cliff edge into the ocean.It changes colour

when music changes.

Ella notices there's the gentle sound of pan pipes consistent with the speed of swirling turquoise. She waits, knowing there's a reason for this journey. She holds her breath.

-        Lela, I want to say something important. I need you to know….

The screen goes black. Nothing. Dead. She taps the keyboard. It fails to respond. She thumps the screen. The next few frantic minutes are spent plugging, unplugging, shouting then screaming at this inanimate object. Her power's out. No signal. She's separated from Fin, can't reach him, suddenly cut off. Trapped in her flat, alone on the A40. The wire is severed. That slender copper wire broken. A careless workman, or a rat scavenging for titbits down the back, near the drains, biting through the casing. Maybe a power surge, too many people relying on the wires to bring them information, the latest score, one too many terminals tripping the connection. Something minor. That's all it takes to rip Lela and Fin apart. A swift, arbitrary, pointless, unforeseen event. It is the same event which forces Ella's hefty form off her chair, squeezes her into a tracksuit and to the threshold of the blue flaked front door. Her heart is hammering, her eyes bleary with tears. She's caught like some struggling insect: fear holds her back, panic pushes her forwards. She knows she must act. She takes a deep breath and steps out past discarded chip papers, into the last of the day's watery sunlight, out, into the muggy fumes of a summer evening.

Kerri Didcot
Miranda Glover

This is your story, Kerri, this is how it is.

You were born in the winter of 1993 on the 14th floor
of an out-of-town hospital on the Oxford ringroad.
You mum, Dee, met your dad at school. They always
chose 16 and 17 on the lotto to match their ages. They
shared pale skin, cheap cigarettes and bad teeth. When
you were born they both still lived at home, ten miles
from the labour ward that delivered you. Huge pylons
ran between their estates like aliens and their houses
had views over the power station that pumped grey
steam into the fuggy air. From Dee's bedroom window
she could peer at passengers on the platforms of the
mainline across the way. All day, every day, at twenty
minute intervals, trains squealed in, doors opened,
people got on and they clunked shut again. Whistles blew
then the passengers were off to the prize-winning villages
lining the river, or up to work in London, which Dee had
never visited. It took under an hour to get to the city but
to your mum it was still a world away.

Jason was your dad. Until Dee took the test he
really hadn't grasped that what they did for kicks would
cause all the trouble to come. When Dee's best friend
Tess announced the news at Broadways Jason turned
white, then he went outside to chunder. Claimed it was
the sixth Stella that did it, but the shock was for real. He

never had much to do with you. Dee's always claimed, "It never made much difference. By the time you were crawling he'd joined the army and by the time you'd hit primary he'd been flown back in a box."

Your memories of your dad are locked in a fading school photo you've got by your bed. He had a lively smile that people who knew him say you share. You've got a wit that's far too sharp for your circumstance. Your nan says that's from Jason too, but how are you to know? You've got your mum's sky blue eyes. They look through people, as if you're sleepwalking towards a future that no one else can see.

Your name is Kerri with an 'i' - Dee said she did it that way 'to be a bit different'. And so you are. Although you like to play it daft your teachers say you've got talent. You're doing 'A' levels: art, English and theatre studies. Your mum says, "You've always been a drama queen," and that she's pleased because, "I get a bit extra from the social for you staying on." But your nan says, "Don't listen to her Kerri, love, Dee's dead proud of you really."

You know that, about your mum, understand that it's tough for her, watching you fulfilling some of her potential. By the time she was your age she'd already left school and had you. She's just turned 32 and could be pretty, but after all those kids... "Not meaning to be rude or anything", your boyfriend, Jamie, says, "But there's a bit too much lard around her thighs". You tell him off for that but you know it's true. Dee hasn't had much luck with men, you, then Keith, then the twins, all with different dads. At least the numbers got her a three-bed up the road from your nan.

Jamie's going to be a mechanic, like his old

man. They'll be in it together; it's a good life. They've got a house on the Ladygrove which Dee calls, "the La-di-da grove" with her eyebrows raised because, "it's got aspirations", mock Georgian three and four beds with white pillars holding up the porches – hundreds of them but no two quite the same. When you go there you secretly think it's not bad. Jamie's mum's really tidy, everything matches, wallpaper and curtains, crockery and cups for tea. Janet's her name. She does nails at the Hairport mornings, but, she says, "I only need to work part-time; Chris keeps me in my shoes."

It's true, Jamie's dad spoils her rotten. Inside their spare room Janet's got a wardrobe full of them: platforms, stilettos, kittens, wedges, flats. "Ready for stepping out in," she giggles, "I can't help it, I get them on eBay." Chris shrugs on the sofa and grins, turns the channel over. As you tell your mum, "It's like Janet plays girly girly in the family, so they all protect her."

Jamie's got an older brother, Stew, who Jamie looks up to. He's a part-time fireman and a fitness instructor. You don't really like all the attention Janet demands from "my three boys". You think there's something fake in her fragile act. Underneath it you reckon she's got a will of steel. You try to put that out of your mind. Sounds jealous and that's the last thing you are. Jamie's washing's always done, tea's on the table at six. "Can't complain," he says with a smirk.

You work at Tesco for extra cash. On school days you're on shift from four to eight. Normally, after, Jamie picks you up in his souped-up Nissan, windows blacked. He says, "It's a long walk home with discount food." Sometimes before you leave he skids you round the car park just for the thrill of it. He's already left school;

didn't see the point. Your shared fate was written before you learned to write. He was the fit one everyone knew, with a skull ring on his middle digit. You were the girl with the feline figure and butterfly eyes.

Jamie wasn't the first. You lost it behind the leisure centre with a boy from Subway on your fourteenth birthday. He shoved you up against the aircon. You closed your eyes and breathed in chlorine from the pool. He used a *Sensation* but for you the experience was pleasure-free. Lately with Jamie you've been experimenting. He likes it oral and you're beginning to enjoy it more. Maybe it's the comfort of the back of his car. And *Jayzee* keeps the rhythm up.

Sometimes after work he drives you out of town and up the hill and parks in the dark. On the horizon the lights from the power station illuminate the steam. You do it in the back, you unbuttoned in your Tesco tunic, Jamie in his overalls, fly undone. While you suck he likes to twist and tug your hair. You always keep some Extras for after, it takes the taste away. Occasionally when you're done Jamie holds your hand and you walk up the hill to look down at the river. You say, "If I got on a boat I wonder where it would take me," then Jamie goes all soft and says, "Away from me, baby. And why the fuck would you wanna do that?"

Until recently you haven't known anyone in the villages around town. Until Jamie got the Nissan you hadn't had any mates with a car. And anyway, there's nothing out there to attract you; all that mud and horses, pubs with open fires, no music or darts. They, however, all think they know you. They rock up at the supermarket in their four-wheel-drives for the half price wines and *Finest* foods. They've noticed you because your eyes really are the most breathtaking blue, you've got that pure white hair and a truly gorgeous smile.

Recently there's been a boy who always waits for your till. Buys chocolate and crisps or bread and milk for his mum. You know his name's Will and that he's 18 because sometimes he buys Red Bull and vodka, which you can't serve so you have to press for someone to check his ID. He never quite looks you in the eye but always mumbles, "How are you?' and then he blushes. He's got long, wavy, dark hair and a narrow face. His look's not common and he lacks the confidence of the boys you know. Once he says, "You look Swedish." You know what he means but as you swipe his clubcard you reply, "Hate swede, used to make us eat it at school." He laughs and finally manages to catch your eye.

It's a Friday and you're on your normal shift. *The Sun* says the weekend's going to be, "a scorcher!" All afternoon as you scan bbq ribs and burgers, monster beers and two-for-one mint choc chip, you think about the summer, stretching wide as a yawn. Jamie wants you to go down Spain with him and Stew, his girlfriend Lorraine, and the parents. A free fortnight's self-catering through a mate from the garage; £300 all in. You've never been abroad. It makes you nervous. Dee says, "Go for it girl." You feel guilty seeing her sitting there with the boys, all they'll be getting is a week on the coast in your nan's static. And you should be saving for college. Instead you went down town before work, bought some clothes to cheer yourself up.

After your shift you wait outside but Jamie doesn't show. He's been learning to fit exhausts. It's still warm and there's a thick silence in the air. You try Jamie's phone twice but he doesn't answer. Finally he texts. "Watching the Brazil game - sorry!" You curse. It's muggy and you've got bags. Last bus leaves at eight. You can see it, on the other side of the car park now, indicating to go.

No choice to walk it. Then a four wheel drive pulls up. Silver. Muddy. Will's behind the wheel. The window's down. *The Killers* are playing. He grins. You smile. Can't help it. Must have just missed him on the tills.

"Want a lift?" he calls.

A ray of sun glints off his windscreen. You scrunch your blue eyes. Think a moment.

"Sure, where you heading?"

"Fancy a drink?"

"Not watching the footie?"

"No, I'm a cricket man," he says.

"Can't go out in my uniform."

"Could drop you home first to change."

You nearly say yes, then think again. You've never felt self-conscious about your house before, but as you glance in at Will sitting there in his *Abercrombie* T-shirt and *Hollister* shorts you know the two won't mix.

"I've got some stuff," you say quickly, lifting the *New Look* bags. "Wait a minute, I'll change."

In the staff toilet you pull off the tags; wriggle into the white denim rara and pink chambray shirt, change your flats for white kittens, add a line of blue kohl under your eyes. Quick squirt of *Impulse* and a comb through your hair, then you practice a grin in the mirror. Prettiness for you is easy but for some reason today you're not sure it's the right kind of pretty.

As you climb up into the car Will's gaze drops briefly to your legs. You try to pull the skirt down over your skinny white thighs and wish you'd booked another

sunbed through Janet. Gets you a discount at the
Hairport. He turns the volume up and heads out of the
car park. With Jamie you always turn right, into town or
up the hill. Will takes a left, towards the villages. You feel
high up. Soft, beige leather seats.

"Nice car," you say.

"My mum's," he replies casually.

"Where do you live?"

"West Stoke."

You nod as if you've been there. No clue really.

"The cricket's on, we can get a drink from the
pub. Sit outside."

"Alright," you say.

The car whirrs and the breeze flays your hair.
The fields blur yellow as Will picks up speed. Soon
he's turning off the ringroad and you're heading down
narrow country lanes. The hedgerows are weighed down
with tiny white flowers; really lovely.

"You still at school?" he asks.

"A levels. You?"

"Just finished."

"What you doing next?"

"Gap Year. Going to save up some money, head
off to Africa in September to work on a reserve. Then
when I get back, Leeds Uni, engineering."

It's the most you've ever heard him say. He
doesn't open his mouth wide when he talks, his accent's
a bit Will Young; soft and posh. He's quite fit in profile.
You search in your bag for some gum. Out of your depth
really.

"I'm working there," he tells you as you pass by
some farm buildings, "To save up for the trip. Really
dirty work, pigs."

You start laughing. It's the last thing you can imagine a posh boy would do. His mouth slopes wryly and you feel your eyelashes flutter.

The village is chocolate box. Thatched cottages, old-fashioned church with a very tall spire. Lots of cars parked up the lane leading to the pub, which is really old, white with tonnes of pink and red geraniums in window boxes. Will squeezes into a space and your door's jammed against the hedgerow.

"Sorry," he says with a sheepish grin, "You'll have to slip over my seat."

As you climb out his eyes slide once more to your legs, then he looks at his feet. For once you wish you'd put on jeans. You walk together down the lane and into the pub garden. Behind it you can see the rec, dotted with men in white. The garden's teeming with people, they're sitting in groups at wooden tables drinking pints, eating crisps. Kids and dogs are running about all over. Some men are standing by the fence, watching the cricket, pints in hands. There's a bunch of lads at a table. One turns, raises a hand and calls out, "Alrigh' Will."

"Alrigh' Tom," he replies.
You wonder what you're doing there. Wish you'd gone straight home. Then Will gives you a warm look and you change your mind. "Drink?" he says.

"Diet coke," you reply and follow him into the pub. Despite the light, it's gloomy inside, dark wooden furniture, low ceilings with beams.

"Not good for really tall people," says Will. Bar's packed. The football's on a big screen in the back bar. Atmosphere's friendly. Will seems to know everyone.

"Your dad says next year you'll be ready for the

firsts," a ruddy man in whites says. Will looks chuffed.

"Is he fielding?" he asks.

"No, in bat," says the man, "Just scored a six. You better get out there and cheer him on."

He winks at you then takes his pint from the bar and ambles back out into the garden.

"Cricket 's a big thing in West Stoke," Will says. He's quite shy, you realise, not just with you, but in general. Must have taken some courage to invite you over. You're wondering what you are going to tell Jamie. You glance down at your phone. No signal. Like the dark ages you think - but secretly you're pleased to be out of range. It's half time and people start piling back outside to have fags and drink their beers.

Will introduces you to his mates, five guys, all a bit like Will, bit messy, longish hair, surf clothes. So not Jamie's style. He'd think they were tossers. One of them sniggers into his beer and another punches him in the arm. You know what it means. Normally, down Broadways, you'd like the attention, but here it makes you feel a bit cheap. Luckily Will keeps his arm up on the table and turns his body towards you, so you're slightly apart from them. That feels exclusive. He wants to know everything, about you and Dee and your brothers and your friends. You find yourself chattering away. But you don't mention Jamie. Something inexplicable stops you. Odd. Normally he's all you ever talk about. When it gets chilly Will puts his sweatshirt round your shoulders and one of his friends says, "What a gentleman," and they all laugh.

The cricketers play until the dusk finally drops then the men move in twos and threes from the rec into the pub. One of them stands at the gate and looks across the tables of drinkers outside, then approaches yours.

"Thrashed 'em!" he says.

"Well done, Dad," says Will, "this is Kerri."

"Hello Kerri," says Will's dad.

Hair's thinning, long face like Will's, twinkling eyes.

"Will, are you going to drive me home? Mum's waiting to eat supper."

They get in the front and you get in the back. You head on up the hill to the outskirts of the village, turn through open gates and up a long, gravel drive. A large, old stone house looms out of the dusk, lights glowing on the ground floor. It's surrounded by trees and lawns with a tennis court. Like a country house hotel. A chocolate-coloured dog bounces at the car as Will's dad opens the passenger door.

"Down, Freddie," he says.

A thin woman in tidy jeans and a white T-shirt has appeared at the doorway. She kisses Will's dad's cheek and takes his cricket bag then looks over at Will.

"Hello, darling. Are you coming in? Supper's ready, there's tonnes. You and your friend are both very welcome."

Will turns and looks at Kerri.

"Hungry?" he says.

Boots and coats fills one side of a large, tiled hall. Red and orange flowers spill from a blue vase. As you pass a wide stairwell you spy a huge oil painting of a man in uniform hanging at the top of it. Your stomach flutters. Dee would go nuts. Forget the Ladygrove. Will was loaded.

You all eat in the kitchen at a long, dark wooden table with no cloth. It's littered with pots of chutney and a plate of foreign-looking cheeses and a bowl of baked potatoes and butter in a glass dish. Will hands round plates from a massive oak dresser. They are large and painted with flowers, each one different to the next. His mum, who introduces herself cheerily as "everyone calls me Bee," gets a big orange casserole dish out of an oven she calls 'the aga' and puts it straight onto the table, announcing; "Beef bourguignon," with a dramatic flourish. Will's dad opens a bottle of red wine.

Bee speaks like Will, soft and warm. She says she had two daughters, Becca and Lou, both away at university,

"I miss their company," she says. "It's lovely to have another beautiful girl in the house for supper. Soon Will will be off too. What will I do?"

"Mum, you're so embarrassing," says Will. "And it's not that bad, you're so busy all the time, and it's not like we were dailies."

"Dailies?"
You can't believe you opened your mouth. Must be the glass of wine.

"We boarded, at school, so we've never exactly been under mum and dad's feet," Will explains between mouthfuls of baked potato.

"You loved it," Bee says defensively.

"I know, I know," says Will. "It wasn't a criticism, just a fact."

"But your mum does miss you when you're all away," says Richard. "Thank god for Freddie, heh." The chocolate dog's by his feet. He gives it a firm pat.

Everyone seems so interested in you tonight. It's not what you're used to, your way or round at Jamie's. By the time you leave you've told them all about your courses and your end of year project on *Tess*.

"Oh I love Hardy," enthuses Bee. "But have you come across Virginia Woolf yet?"

You shake your head.

"Start with *To The Lighthouse*," she says. "I'll help you. To begin with you might find her style challenging. But once you're in the rhythm you won't look back."

Bee's up from her chair and vanishes for a moment.

"Mum's always like this," says Will and Richard laughs. "She teaches English part time," he adds, "You've got her right on her favourite topic."

Bee reappears moments later with a very slim volume and hands it to you. There's a drawing of a woman who looks a bit like a horse in an old fashioned hat on the cover. You feel yourself blush but you are happy.

Later you get Will to drop you at the roundabout. He takes your number and you say thank you but luckily he doesn't try to kiss you or grope you or any of that. What would Jamie say? Even so, as you get out of the car a part of you feels disappointed that he didn't ask to see you again. You walk the last bit down the back alley. Didn't want him coming any closer. And anyway, you needed time to think it through. Tonight felt as foreign as a week on the Costa del Sol, and you'd only been a few minutes' drive away from all that is familiar. Just goes to show what you don't know. Virginia Woolf's in your pocket; like it's burning a hole. Now you're heading past the pylons and there's the power station ahead of you and the railway track and the little row of council houses that you know as home and the evening's beginning to feel like a dream. Like someone else's life. And you feel a bit ashamed of the whole thing.

"Jamie's been looking for you," says Dee.

She's got one eye on the telly, sips her tea.

102

"He didn't pick me up, I've been down the pub."

"World Cup's on," she says.

"Mum," you say.

"What is it, love?"

"I don't think I'll go down Spain."

"Don't worry about me and the boys, we're fine here. Go, love, get a bit of life experience."

"No," you say, "I've thought about it. I just don't want to go."

Days pass and become a week. Everything you do seems paler than it was a while ago, even though the sun gets hotter every day and the nights grow longer and with the heat turning up Jamie's appetite for you gets stronger, voracious some would say, well, not round your way maybe, but perhaps as Bee would say. Yes, it's true, it's her you're thinking about as much as Jamie.

You started *To the Lighthouse* in bed the night she gave it to you, after you made the decision about Spain. It's now the following Sunday, only ten past eight, but you're lying on your bed reading. The final's on and Jamie's watching it up Broadways. You didn't feel like the crowd, the noise. You don't understand the book really but Bee was right, there's a rhythm in the writing that touches a chord in you; the voices and their stories ebb and flow through the lines, like living and dreaming all at the same time. It makes you feel apart, like being apart. You don't tell anyone about it, read before you sleep then hide it under your pillow. It's thin enough not to stop you sleeping. Jamie wouldn't understand it, would just think you wanted to go out with Will. He wouldn't understand how a book could be a way to love.

Shauna Bristol

"But Shauna rather liked the clockman. She liked the care he took over things, the way he concentrated so intensely on that clock, shining it and winding it and talking to it under his breath as if it was a living, breathing thing."

Lucy Cavendish

Shauna Bristol
Lucy Cavendish

Tick Tock. Tick Tock. Shauna looked at the grandfather clock marking time in the hallway. She'd always had ambiguous feelings about that clock. It made her feel late, constantly late, as if time were running out on her. It didn't really help that her father insisted it run ten minutes slow. "I like it that way," he said ruffling slightly when Shauna pointed out that most people kept their clocks running fast so that they would never be late for anything. "Who wants to be on time?" her father would say, pretending to yawn. "So pedestrian!" She knew his deliberately lax attitude towards keeping the clock just so drove the rather serious clockman mad.

He'd come every four months in his tidy grey suit, pull up in the drive in his little white van and then appear neatly on the dot at the doorway holding his mending bag. Even as a child observing him labouring over the magnificent timepiece, Shauna could see how it's tardiness annoyed him, and how he tried to repress gasps of frustration at its enforced delay. She'd see the muscles on his back inadvertently tense up when his immaculately kept wrist watch, or 'timepiece' as the clockman used to call it, told him it was 8pm or whatever, and the grandfather didn't ring out for another ten minutes. It obviously drove him silently mad. "Want me to put it right Mr C?" the clockman would ask every time, but Shauna's father would dismiss him with a casual wave of his hand. "Obviously not," he'd say, looking at the clock man as if he were a complete idiot. "I like being late. It means you can make an entrance, you see. Not that I suppose you'd know much about that."

Shauna always thought this rude. Why didn't her father speak more courteously to the poor man? She imagined it was because he found him – as he found many things – boring. Her father usually had two reactions to people. He either found them immediately dull and virtually ignored them completely or he'd be enamoured of them for a short period of time and then, like a particularly malicious cat, dispatch them back to their tedious little lives having played his mean set of mind games on them.

The clockman fell in to the first category, Shauna thought. The clock was run slow to irritate everyone. When they used to have house guests, which became rarer and rarer, her father would delight in not telling them about this quirk of the clock. He'd call for dinner at 8pm and then become hysterical and riled when everyone came to the dining room ten minutes late. "I said eight o'clock!" he'd yell, huffing and puffing like a cross peacock. "Not ten minutes later." But then, when everyone finally sat down looking suitable sheepish, he'd eventually let them off the hook and reveal his secret. "The clockman can't bear it," he'd say. "Drives him mad but amuses me my darlings," and then everyone would laugh away, voices tinkling off the chandeliers.

But Shauna rather liked the clockman. She liked the care he took over things, the way he concentrated so intensely on that clock, shining it and winding it and talking to it under his breath as if it was a living, breathing thing. Everything with the clockman seemed ordered somehow. Sometimes he brought his son, a small pale boy probably not much older than Shauna. The boy sat solemnly in the corner, refusing to look at anyone, only at the clock, while his father tended to it, and moving only when his father asked him for some help.

"Hold this," the clockman would say and the little boy would get up and take whatever delicate instrument his father was offering to him. Shauna noticed how large the tools looked in his small hands. He had freckled, milk-coloured skin with small slightly ginger hairs on his pale naked arms that stretched out like matchsticks from the cuffs of his nicely ironed white short-sleeved school shirt. The boy seemed to love the clock as much as his father did. But once when he came he saw Shauna's father in such a purple rage – ranting and panting and swearing – that he ran and hid back in the van. The clockman didn't though. Amidst the rain of expletives that rained down from about – "Those dullards, those Jeremiads, those nay Sayers, those…Why is everyone so bloody boring?" He carried on with his job. But that was the last time he came. Shauna asked her father about it once but all he said was, "He irritated me and that clock doesn't need him." Conversation closed.

Shauna also loved the clock sometimes. Its ticking and chiming seemed to mark off various turning points in her life, a somehow reassuring presence in the whirling, twirling scenes of emotions, of which there had been so many in this house. The clock just carried on marking it all out, the repetitive, monotonous sound of familiarity. When her father fell down the stairs - "so careless to fall down the stairs, so unfair" - and a small shard of glass from his cracked spectacles dislodged and pierced his eye and he lay there still, like a victim from a murder scene, a body that was waiting for the police to come and draw lines round it, the clock just carried on ticking. Then, when her father had recovered slightly and finally come home to convalesce – grumbling all the way and fumbling for Shauna's hand like a blind man without a stick – he'd gone to sleep with a lit cigarette dangling from his hand and set fire to his armchair so much so that smoke filled the house and it all nearly burned down. Tock said the clock.

The morning after the fire, as her father was once again back in hospital and Shauna had gone to see quite how singed his nostril hair was, he claimed the fire had nothing to do with him.

"I did not fall asleep!" he said indignantly. "That fire was nothing to do with me. So irritating to have a fire."

Shauna just sat and looked at him. She was used to it now, the dark denials, the rush of hot protestation, his complaints of being endlessly and futilely bored. She knew that, soon, he'd either be weeping like an abandoned child looking for its mother or fast asleep, snoring gently, no doubt dreaming of a land whereby everything was so much more interesting than this one. Shauna had told him, in a bout of rare and enforced energy, that she could barely muster around her father, that if she hadn't have come in from her job as a temp early that night and fought her way through a cloud of darkening ash and bits of armchair that were swirling out of the door, sucked skywards by the fresh air, he would be dead. Tick. Tock.

They both knew he didn't care.

110

"Why didn't you just leave me there?" her father said. "Why didn't you just leave me there to die?" Shauna almost told him that she'd thought about it, considered for a moment not calling the fire brigade to dampen the flames licking up the side of the chair. And anyway, she thought, he almost had died. She'd had to slap him in the face hard, amazed that he was still breathing, then drag him out of the room and throw a coal scuttle of water on the smouldering chair. .

As her father had become increasingly ill, she'd taken to watching out for him. For years she would come home to find him sitting at the window in the hall, watching life go by and listening to the tick tock of the clock. She understood why. There really wasn't anything else for him to do. His friends had left him now, all gone away, too embarrassed to spend time with this person who once charmed them most. Her father claimed to find them all as dull as ditch water.

"Not a single original thought amongst them!" he'd say as he lit another cigarette, not noticing that there was already one gently smouldering away in the overlarge glass ashtray. When Shauna once pointed out he'd already lit three in the space of a minute, he looked at her with such affront that she never dared say anything again and gradually she'd almost stopped noticing the endless abandoned cigarettes lying incinerated but not really smoked in rows around the rim of the ashtray.

All her father could do in the days of his failing health was wait for the Chinese man who washed the cars next door to stop by the window and have a chat. In the earlier years, when they still had hope, he would spend weeks in clinics round the countryside. Sometimes, morose and miserable, he would volunteer to go in.

"I'm nothing more than an embarrassment," he'd say, moving shambolically across the room trying to persuade his packed suitcase to rise off the floor with only one feeble hand. Shauna would never say anything then. She didn't know what to say. Yes, you're an embarrassment was too mean, too strong. But to say no was..well..false. Other times she would have to persuade him, kicking and screaming, in to the taxi . "You know you need to go," she'd say, ignoring the kerfuffle he was making. She would do anything to get him in to the vehicle that was going to take him away to a place in the countryside where there would be no alcohol, lots of people to talk to and crap food.

He never lasted long. He charmed everyone from the cook to the counsellor. Whatever she took away from him – his clothes, his walking stick, even his glasses, he found a way of persuading someone to get him back home. He'd reappear, as if he'd never left, and open up a bottle of whisky. Tick tock. "So awful that clinic,' he'd say petulantly.

Now, of an evening, he was no longer there and the house was an empty echoing shell, Shauna sometimes did exactly the same thing her father used to do. She sat at the window and watched the world go by. There was the posh old lady from across the square who walked her tiny Pomeranian very slowly, the dog defecating as it went. There was the Italian man, with matching tan belt and shoes, who strode past always at 6pm as if he had somewhere to go but Shauna had no idea where it was. There was nothing to do in the square. No offices, no pub, just big beautiful houses that people with money owned.

Nothing ever changed. Time passed. Shauna

wondered if any of those people who went by the house and looked up at its blank windows missed her father sitting in his chair. She wondered if they'd ever noticed him being there. But then again, as he had become increasingly frail, he'd stopped sitting there. He'd just taken to his room and Shauna had put a television in there for him and that was what he did day-in, day-out, lay and watched TV.

Tick. Tock. So, on this day, this day of all days, Shauna stood in the hallway of her father's house and looked at the clock. Tick. Tock. Tick. Tock.

"Nothing's going to be the same again," she said to it. "Nothing."

They were coming today, the people, the endless people her father would never have had time for. That's why she was there. It was time she said her goodbyes to the house and the clock and everything else that went with it. She looked at her father's bed. She thought of him dying in it. He hadn't said anything. It wasn't as if he'd had a conversion, nothing like that at all and she hadn't really expected it. She'd sat there on that warm, almost peculiarly hot evening and held his hand but his eyes had been closed and, as the hours went by, he sort of shrunk. His breath grew shallow and raspy and his skin seemed to thin out under her gaze. She'd called her brothers then. Come, she said. He's about to go.

By the time they'd got there, it was too late. But it didn't matter. He was still warm and everyone talked to him and no one seemed to mind that he couldn't hear. Two nights later, she'd taken a man she'd only met once before and fucked him on that bed. The man was dark and beautiful but she barely knew him and she didn't think, at the time, that it mattered really although it was totally out of character for her. The rest of her family were next door, gathered round the kitchen table drinking whisky and reminiscing and trying to pretend they couldn't hear what was going on.

"We all deal with grief in different ways." That was what her brother said through the thin wall. But Shauna didn't think it was grief. She thought it was payback.

The sting was in the will of course. His final wishes. Shauna had been waiting for it, expecting there to be a chink of something left open just to make sure that nothing could not be divided without causing rancour. Her younger brother had gone on and on about it for days.

"What do you think he'll have left us?" he kept on saying. He even talked about it at the funeral, as if it were nothing more than an inconvenience to have to break that pattern of thought to inter their father's ashes in the ground.

"Nothing," Shauna would say some days, vaguely, then, in the next moment, "everything."

It was being taken away today, the clock. That was the sting. The children could have whatever they wanted from his personal effects, but they'd have to pay for it. He had stipulated it in the will. Every single item was to have a price put on it and it would all go to an auction house and they would have to bid to get it back. So clever. So cruel. Tick. Tock.

Men, faceless, nameless men, had been and visited the house with their plummy accents and faux friendliness. But, to Shauna, they'd been like gannets, rifling with their demanding, inquisitive fingers through the most personal of stuff. The paintings, rugs, armoire, the antique bed, the not-so antique bed, even down to that glass ashtray, had been examined over and over again as the men did little calculations in their brains. It had been Shauna's job to show them round. They asked questions, endless questions. Where had that chair come from? How old was it? When did the monkey from the monkey band in the display case lose the tip of its ear? They rejected the half-burnt out armchair Shauna noticed. Her father had refused to part with it and now it wasn't even wanted.

The men took her memories and put a price on them. They got to the clock last of all. Shauna knew how they felt before any of them even opened their mouths.

"What a beautiful piece," one of them said. "Does it run true?" Shauna looked at them and smiled.

"Oh yes,' she said. "It's utterly accurate." When they took it, she cried quietly and unnoticed from behind the front door.

Two days later Shauna found herself on a small City bus careering through Fishponds. It was typical of her father to be so difficult. Instead of finding a reputable auction house in the centre of town, he'd left it all to be sold in a warehouse on the outskirts. Shauna could hear him saying it now, "so much more interesting to get out and about my dear." She had no idea who would traipse this far out just to look at her father's effects. Her brothers had made it clear that they wanted nothing other than the money.

"I can't really think of anything I'd like," they both said. For Shauna it was different. She wanted to see the faces of the people who bought the bookcases and chairs and porcelain figures. These are my father's things, she thought. They have meaning to me. She somehow wanted to tell the people about him, tell them how many cigarettes per hour he'd stub out in the ashtray that some other person would now possess.

As Shauna thought about her father she felt so angry she clutched the handkerchief in her pocket and nearly ripped it in two. Then, suddenly, she thought she was going to cry so she blinked rapidly. Entering the auction house, she realized she'd spent half her life in Bristol. She needed a change, she thought as she took her seat at the back of the room. She felt too nervous to sit at the front. She looked around her. There were more people here than she'd expected. This did not bode well. Shauna had tried to kid herself she was here to observe but, as she took her seat, she realized she was kidding herself. She was here for a purpose. Shauna thumbed the catalogue marking the items she wanted. She looked at the wad of notes tucked in her handbag. She had saved up. She thanked her lucky stars for her prudence, a prudence that had been inherited from nowhere she could think of.

She sighed and made a little prayer. Dear God, she said, please help me buy the things that should be mine. Please.

An hour later, it was obvious God was not on her side. Lot 3, a walnut dresser she had always loved and which had sat beside her father's bed ever since she could remember, went for £3000, way over the £500 Shauna had earmarked for it. Lot 10, an ottoman that used to sit unused and unloved in a bathroom at the top of the house, went for £1000. Lot 16, the bronze sculpture of "Puss" had fetched £2000. She'd never understood why her father had bought it. He didn't even like cats, or any animals for that matter. She had decided that he must have been in one of his Machiavellian moods when he bought it as he had unveiled it to her one night and, noting her look of surprised disappointment, announced it had cost 'thousands'.

"It's very middle class to worry about money," he'd said.

Shauna put her head in her hands. This was a disaster. She decided she'd concentrate on who the buyers were. Lot 20, the oak wardrobe from her father's bedroom that she had assumed was worth no more than, say £250 at a push, went for three times that to an intense woman with glasses on. Lot 25, five books about the River Thames, went for £500 more than the men in suits thought they should have done. A man wearing a beret bought them. And a tall, attractive man with a mop of fair hair wearing a tweed jacket was eyeing the page in the catalogue that had her father's antique four-poster bed, the round wooden dining table and a Messian China monkey band. Shauna stared at him intensely. Something about him was familiar but she couldn't place him. Was he an antique dealer? Had she once wandered into his shop? Maybe he came from Bath. There were loads of antique shops in Bath. She couldn't remember. But then she realized he wasn't bidding on anything, just waiting. Tick. What was he waiting for? Tock.

An hour later, Shauna decided she had to have a strategy. She had managed to buy nothing more than one bedside lamp from her old bedroom for £50 and the whole process had made her blush. She has raised her catalogue and waved it around frenetically and everyone had stared at her, including attractive tweed-jacket man. The auctioneer had pointed to her and called her, "the blonde lady at the back." She had not dared

117

move since. Everything was going for too much money anyway. Seeing her father's life laid out before her in the catalogue she decided she would just bid all out on the one thing she really wanted. It would be hers even if it meant spending all the £2,500 in one go.

Eventually, lot 130 was up. "Grandfather clock," said the auctioneer, staring round the room. "Shall we start the bidding at £50?" Shauna waved her catalogue in the air. "£50 to the blonde lady at the back," said the auctioneer. "Do I hear £100?" The intense lady with the glasses on raised her hand. The beret-wearing man raised to £150. "Do I hear £200?" asked the auctioneer. Shauna raised her catalogue again but she was quickly trumped by the intense lady. On they went, the three of them, until Shauna raised the bid to £1000. "Do I hear more than £1000?" said the auctioneer. There was a pause. "I've got it!" thought Shauna. But then the intense lady bid £1,500. The beret-wearing man bid £2000. Shauna raised to £2,500. She had reached her limit.

For a moment, time stood still. All she heard was ringing in her ears. Then the intense lady raised to £3000. "£3000, going, going…" Shauna waved her catalogue. God, how was she going to find £3,500? But she couldn't stop. It was a challenge set down to her by her father. She could hear him now, her asking him in a plaintive voice, "I'm a thousand pounds short" and him replying, "don't be so boring Shauna. Always so boring!"

The intense-lady raised to £4000. Shauna sat there, the hand that was holding her catalogue felt as heavy as lead. "Go on!" her father's voice said in her head. "Why did you think I did this? For you to do something with your life Shauna. Just do it, wave that hand. Rob a bank, whatever it takes. Buy that clock." But

Shauna just sat there. Tears began to form in her eyes. He was here now, in this room, her father. She could smell him, that stale alcohol and cigarettes on his breath. He was angry now. She could feel it.

"£10,000!" The voice rang out.

Shauna whipped round, her father's voice disappearing as quickly as it came. It was the blond man.

"£10,000, final offer," he said.

He was looking straight at the auctioneer. £10,000! Shauna's eyes started smarting. The auctioneer turned to look at her. He raised his eyebrows. Shauna shook her head, as did the intense-looking lady. Then, in tears, Shauna ran from the auction room. The double doors banged as she left.

Shauna was jolted out of her thoughts by the ringing of the doorbell. It made her jump. No one had been to the house in weeks. All the items had gone, left home, shipped off and out like unwanted children to boarding school. It was sold anyway. She'd just come to pick up a few final things as the new owners had asked for the house to be totally cleared, a dusty bottle of wine that she found in the cupboard under the stairs, a few old plates, a train track in the attic covered in cobwebs. The doorbell rang again. Oh fuck off, Shauna thought. It was probably another gannet looking for some debris to pick over, though why anyone would want to come to this sad house on a night like this, Shauna had no idea. She could hear the singing coming from the pub. It had started as she had walked to the house. She knew it would get louder; kick off was about to happen. She resolved to be out of the house before the end of the match. She was in no mood for drunken revellers.

There was a blonde man standing on the

doorstep. Shauna recognised him immediately from the auction house. She smiled, nervously, not sure what else to do.

"Do you want to come in she said, caught off guard, "or…"

"Or what?" he asked.

Shauna shrugged, "Go to the pub, watch the match."

"I'm not interested in that," he said. Then he looked at her intensely.

"You don't remember me do you?"

"Yes I do. You were at the auction. You bought…"

"The clock?'

Shauna nodded.

"Yes, the clock."

The man smiled at her.

"You met me a few times in this house," he said, 'When we were children. You used to sit in the corner of the sitting room and I'd sit in the other and watch everything…your father, a difficult man I think…"

"Oh my God," Shauna said, "you're the clockman!"

"Son of the clockman," he corrected her.

"Yes, of course! Now I know where I saw you before. I knew it in the auction house but I couldn't place you. It's been years."

"I know. My father stopped coming. I think he couldn't bear it."

Shauna gave a short laugh. "Well, that was my father for you. He found looking after anything rather…"

"Boring?" said the man.

"Yes,' said Shauna, smiling slightly. 'Boring is probably the right word."

They looked at each other for a while.

"Well, I think you should come outside."
Shauna looked at him doubtfully.

"No, it's fine," he said. "I don't bite. Just… come."
Shauna followed him as he walked down the short path to the road. Parked in front of the house was a large white van.

"I have something for you," he said.

"No," said Shauna. She thought she was going to cry. "No."

The man took her hand gently in his. "Yes,' he said "Yes. It's for you. It was always yours and I want you to have it back.. I know how hard it was for you. I've thought about it for years, that torture he put you through."

"It was just him," she said but suddenly she felt she was about to break down. "I don't have the money. I can't afford to buy it off you."

"I didn't ask you to buy it."

"But why?" Shauna asked him, blinking back tears as he went to open the van.

"Because," he said.

"That's not good enough."

"Because I saw what he was like and I wanted you to have something that gave you good thoughts not bad. I just wanted to buy it for you and when I saw you there…."

Shauna shook her head.

"I can't accept it. It's too much. I know how much you paid for it and, I just can't."
The man looked at her, and then he said, very slowly, "Yes you can Shauna. Go on. I bought it for you. It's a

gift. It's really that simple because, not everything has to be complicated."

And as he opened the door, the clock started chiming.

"Eight o'clock," he said, taking Shauna's hand more firmly now and drawing her towards the van.

"No," she said, feeling the warmth of his palm in hers. "Oh, you've forgotten haven't you? After all this time…Don't you remember? It always ran slow. It's actually ten past eight."

Meredith *London*

"The bar is heaving. Bodies overflowing from the doorway, drowning the place in boisterous shouts and ribaldry. There are several screens showing the build-up to the game."

Jennie Walmsley

Meredith London
Jennie Walmsley

The Underground smells of a thousand festering male armpits. And diesel. Is it diesel? Meredith doesn't really know, it's that oily smell. It can't be diesel, for God's sake, this is the 21st century and even London's underground trains are driven by electricity, so what is that? It reminds her of when she used to hang around at the junk yard in sixth form. The older brother of one of her friends was renovating a scooter. She'd flirted a lot with him and it had worked, and she'd lost her virginity to him, and the whole thing had lasted about two months, which at the time had seemed a big deal. That was nearly fifteen years ago. She hardly ever thinks about him now. Strange how odours can summon the past.

The tube lurches and she collides in to the man standing next to her. He's stocky, with a sore looking red neck that reminds her of a bull. He stands firm as she bounces off him. He's a side of beef, immoveable in his solidity. Her mumbled apology is met with a watery, red eyed grin. She hates him, and all she wants to do is get off this bloody train, and get to the pub and order a long cold drink and sit down with a bit of space around her. She feels suffocated by masculinity, men's bodies compacted around her, sucking up the limited supply of warm oxygen on the train and depriving her of it. They're all in high spirits. If not drunk already, well on their way or frantic to be so, to lose themselves in the oblivion. And with only half an hour to go, they're beginning to panic they won't have soaked up enough alcohol before kick-off. Sometimes she wonders at the differences between men and women, their motivations. Like now, even with all the hoohah of the last few weeks, the endless matches, and debates and coverage and parties and replays, she can still only see it as a game involving twenty-two men and a ball. But for some of the guys in the office, you'd think it was of critical, life-changing importance. Even Lawrence, she suspects will be utterly absorbed by the TV for much of the evening.

The average male ejaculation contains an estimated hundred million sperm. The likelihood of fertilisation of an egg is dependent on the sperm's motility (the rate and way in which they move)and morphology (whether or not they are well-formed). Even if there is plentiful healthy sperm, each woman of child-bearing age usually only produces one egg per month capable of being fertilised within a limited forty-eight hour timescale. Should such a woman have intercourse with a man during this period, and his ejaculate be of the fittest grade, there is a 40% chance of fertilisation. Given these statistics, it may come of something of a surprise to know that at any one time in the UK an estimated million women are pregnant.

What if she's growing a man, a boy, a male? How weird would it be to be creating something so similar and yet so other? She knows it's pathetic, but over the last few days she's been wondering at the weirdness of growing a willy inside her. Women's bits she can just about imagine. A Russian doll of a baby, like her, just smaller. But something that could grow up into a hairy oaf, with testicles? An odd thought. One that makes her feel slightly, pathetically queasy. She's bought herself a book. It felt like buying porn. It's in her bag, and she's been sneaking looks at it all day. It has diagrams of her insides and pictures of how the embryo develops. The foetus is currently about the size of a cashew nut. Not dissimilar in appearance either, top heavy and rolled in on itself.

She can't believe it won't be a girl. Maybe with Lawrence's thick hair, or his perhaps his skin tone, more olive than hers, but otherwise herself again. A mini-me. It would be strange to have a baby that didn't even look like her, though she's heard it is common for newborns to resemble their fathers.

In their journal article "Mother and Child Bonding" (Human Development, Cambridge University Press, Vol 6, 2008) Anglusch and Baxter investigated the hypothesis that within their first year infants more closely resemble fathers than mothers. This idea enjoys widespread anecdotal support, with at least three of the five leading UK-based parenting magazines running articles on the issue within the last year. Anglusch and Baxter conducted a survey in which they showed two thousand individuals photographs of a selection of 9 to 12 month old babies, women (the mothers) and men (the fathers). When asked to match babies with their parents, babies were found twice as likely to be correctly matched with their mothers as their fathers. A similar result was found for infants of less than three months. Anglusch and Baxter hypothesised that the notion of infants most clearly resembling their fathers was a myth used to insist upon, or embed, paternity and male parental responsibility.

The crowd surges forward on to the platform

as soon as the doors open. A greedy rush of individual ambition to be out of the vacuum of the carriage, and up the stairs before anyone else. The shove of the crowd, bursting from the train's confines, elbows jagged, horizontal, racing one another in slightly over-emphasised movement. Just to get to the end of the platform before anyone else, to conquer the stairs, reach the ticket barrier first, not get waylaid on the way to the pub by idiots who haven't got their Oyster cards out in time. Why don't they all slow down a bit? What is this obsession with speed? Meredith takes a deep breath and pointedly stops to help a large black woman negotiate the stairs with her bags, pushchair and sleeping two-year old. She hasn't noticed before but there's no lift at Queens Park. The woman smiles weakly at Meredith, muttering her thanks towards the ground. That London thing, where strangers find it hard to acknowledge each other; a slight anxiety at getting involved.

Meredith doesn't care much anyway. She's more concerned about the time. She said she'd be at the bar by six thirty. She's late, and she knows it will be crowded. Her shirt is sticking to her, her bag's heavy. She feels laden down, as if incapable of moving forwards. It's not just the end of a tiring day, it's the heavy humidity pressing down on her. She feels susceptible to the weather, like a barometer.

Many pregnant women report an increased sensitivity to fluctuations in the weather in the early days of pregnancy. Increased body temperature and consequential sweating is particularly acute during sleep: a condition known as "nocturnal hyperhydrosis". This can result in lethargy and fatigue. In addition to raised temperatures, sensitivity to air pressure

is magnified with more frequent migraines being
reported during sunnier or more humid weather. Body
temperature change is only one of the reported
physical symptoms of the first trimester. Other
conditions include nausea, tenderness of the breasts,
oedema, increased breathlessness, a greater
sensitivity to smell, general fatigue, weight gain,
constipation.....

The bar is heaving. Bodies overflowing from the
doorway, drowning the place in boisterous shouts and
ribaldry. There are several screens showing the build-up
to the game. A cacophony of commentary, supposition
and posturing. How is it women are thought of as gossips
and opinion mongers, she wonders. Surely there are only
so many ways to kick a ball into the back of a net.

She launches through the crowd, hunching
herself down to squeeze between bodies which hardly
acknowledge her presence. Usually this proximity
to strange men would merit attention, but they are
preparing for war, their minds on higher things, the
great God of football consuming their attention.
One hand swiftly brushes over her backside, but it is
unidentifiable. Perhaps an accidental sweep, certainly
not conversational. She wonders when she will begin to
"show" and therefore become sexually invisible. She's
seen it with friends, and her elder sister, Imogen, the way
in which the growth of a bump gradually "rubs out" a
woman's sexual presence. Is there something territorial
about it? One of the men in the office had joked about
"not pissing where other dogs piss". She hadn't like the
analogy and she hadn't even been pregnant at the time.

One of the things she likes about working in her
agency is the sometimes crude honesty of her colleagues,

131

but she worries that it's an honesty only shared amongst young, beautiful people. She's seen what can happen when women go off and leave work to have kids. How few of them come back to the agency, and if they do, how they're treated. Not quite so interesting, somehow. Certainly less physically taught: "fatter" you might say. She smiles at herself. A kind of knowledge that she's embarked on something that's going to separate her from her colleagues, but it's still secret. At the meeting on Friday, when they'd been discussing the launch of next summer's range, she was making calculations about dates, and realised she'd miss it. That's if she combined maternity leave with annual leave. She catches sight of Lawrence, in the garden, his back towards her, he's staring intently at a large screen which has been erected against the far wall. He glances around, catches her eye, smiles, waves his bottle in acknowledgement and gestures to ask if she can get a round in. She smiles and nods. She pushes through to the bar, miraculously catching the bartender's eye.

"Pint of lime soda and a Corona," she half shouts, half mimes.

It's as if she's swimming through sound. Like the roar of the sea when you're pulled under a wave. She wonders whether it will be too noisy to talk to Lawrence after all. She doesn't want to be shouting at him. It had seemed a good idea to arrange to have a drink and chat things through, begin to make some decisions. She needs a commitment from him. She needs to know this week if she should pull out of buying the flat with Lauren. The mortgage offer is about to expire, and she needs to sort out where she'll be living from September onwards given that she's already told her landlord she's leaving.

The "bean", as she's taken to calling it, has changed everything. Lawrence's support needs to be translated into something tangible. His flat's not going to be big enough, he'll have to sell, probably before they can buy, unless she can get a bridging loan, or Mum and Dad kick in. There's a slow pulse of tension travelling up from her shoulders to her temples, a dull throb reaching inside her head, slowly absorbing her brain. She catches sight of herself in the mirror behind the bar as she's trying to rub it away, her hand moving in gentle circular motions across her forehead and down the side of her cheek. For a fraction of a second she sees Mum reflected rather than herself, the pale skin, hair brushed back behind her ears, a long fringe flopping forwards, a certain tightness around the jawline.

She pays for the drinks, swigs a big mouthful, the reflection reassuringly melting back into herself. She's feels a little faint. Maybe she needs something to eat, a bit of energy. She keeps flitting between desperate hunger and nausea at the thought of food. Fresh air might be better. She carefully takes the glass in one hand and bottle in the other to battle back to the garden. She could move into Lawrence's at the end of the summer until he's sold, though she'll need somewhere to store her things. His place should go on the market as soon as possible if they're to catch the summer window. She wonders whether she could get the same mortgage deal if Lawrence were to take Lauren's place. The offer was based on her working full-time, but she doesn't know yet what she'll want to do about working. Ideally, she'd go part-time, but she knows that's pretty frowned upon. There's lip-service to flexible working, but all the women who've gone part-time whilst she's been there have "chosen" to leave within a year of coming back to work. Couldn't make the finances add up or felt they weren't being given challenging enough projects. Lawrence gets up when she reaches him. He takes the bottles off her, puts his other arm around her back and pulls him in towards him, kissing her full on the lips.

"Hi, gorgeous."

A woman's earnings diminish by 4 percent for every year she is away from paid employment. Given the limited and expensive range of childcare available, many women opt to go part-time after the birth of a child, but in so doing they often move themselves to a lower paid sector of the work market. By becoming a mother, a woman is likely to diminish her overall earnings by a fifth, in addition to having an impact on her pension earnings.

She wants to talk to him about flat options before the game starts, but she can already see that Gary Linekar's full-flow pre-match analysis has seduced Lawrence. It will be nearly impossible to drag his concentration back from the chants resounding around Jo'burg to the price of maisonettes in North West London. The crowds are waving huge flags, and there's that curious mass animal sound of roaring fans. Faces, thick with tribal war paint, leer out of the screen. They're strangely only half human. Allegiances and identities, and all of these people around the world watching and chanting and hoping. Her thoughts flicker to the imaginary garden, the one with a postage stamp of sky under which she could park a buggy. A few pots with plants, room for a sandpit, maybe even a climbing frame. She can feel herself racing ahead, she knows

"Just ten more minutes," Lawrence shouts back, holding up his fingers to help her understand.

"I'm bursting. Don't let 'em score," she stands up just as the crowd moves forward in a synchronised surge of excitement.

Full bladder, full bladder, full bladder…the thought rolls around in her head. She's flushing hot and cold, and wonders whether she might be coming down with something. The hammer inside her head is thumping really hard.

She pauses at the loo and examines the door which is scratched with obscene graffiti. Images she hasn't seen for a while. It smells of beer and lily of the valley air freshener inside the cubicle. She closes the door and rests her head against its cool, varnished surface. And then she pulls down her knickers and sits on the loo and looks down. And that's when she sees all the blood.

8

Linda _Manchester_

"_It was her choice to choose
not to open it. And choice
was not a word she used
often. Linda had always felt
that life moved in ways over
which she had little control.
Her life. A black and white
silent movie. She had sat
there watching it helplessly._"

Anne Tuite-Dalton

Linda Manchester
Anne Tuite-Dalton

Six weeks after her 48th birthday in the evening on July 11th Linda Parson changed the lock of her front door. When she had finished she put the two screwdrivers neatly back into the toolbox and wrapped the now useless and tarnished heavy metal implement along with the few rusty screws still dangling from it into the morning copy of News of the World. The water trickled slowly on her hands and she cleaned them carefully. There should be no grease left beneath her short fingernails. She looked at the clock on the microwave. It was ten past eight.

She didn't sit down for a cup of tea as usual after a job like this. Instead she took the strange parcel and went to her bedroom where she put it in the bottom drawer of her bedside table. There was a large suitcase from under her bed. She packed it with all of Andy's belongings. The night before she had methodically tidied everything up. Nothing of his should be left behind. She didn't sit on the bed at any point to smell his jumper one last time nor did she hesitate when removing his shaving things and toothbrush from the ledge on top of the basin. The worn soft leather bulged in parts when she fastened the buckles. She carried the case into the kitchen and left it by the front door.

In the cupboard where she kept the broom and the hoover there was a heap of large square plastic bags of the kind you have to buy from Sainsbury's. Her manager had given her a few dusty ones the last time they had cleared the till area. She took one out and unfolded it. In the lounge she knelt by the television. He had wanted to buy a new one when he had moved in a year ago but she had refused. The room was small and she didn't want one of those enormous screens in the middle of it. As it was the only proper contribution he had offered to make there was nothing sizeable that she needed to pack. The bag was soon full of DVDs neatly piled on top of each other. Behind the door was a shoe rack. Two pairs were his. She picked them up gingerly and deposited them in the plastic bag.

The job wasn't quite done yet. Once a haven from the day's ups and downs, her bedroom had become a room where she feared going. It was hard to believe that from tonight it would be hers and hers only once again. His night shift ended at 5 and his weight usually fell upon her half an hour later.

Linda stripped the sheets and replaced them with crisp white ones that had not been used for a long time. It already looked different. Andy's shirt or trousers were not hanging on the chair. And they would not be anymore. The floor would not be littered every night with crumpled socks and underwear. The bright red numbers on the clock would allow time to roll gently by again. They would stop being the constant reminder that as the night unfolded, his return drew nearer.

She stood up. She must be on the move now. She put on a light jumper and laden with the suitcase and the bag she left the flat. It was a Sunday so there were not many buses. But hers was on time and the roads were not too busy. The man in the lobby of the security firm where he worked let her in.

"These are for Andy. Andy Stocks." She put down the bag and suitcase. "He works in the central monitoring department."

"And this too, please." In her hand an A4 sheet of paper folded up. A note written the night before. "Please can you let him know it's there., it's important." He looked at her and nodded then his eyes wandered back to the television screen. As she stepped outside she stopped and looked around. She breathed in and out. Slowly. The rain had stopped. The outside world looked metallic and clean.

The bus was empty and the driver nodded kindly as she got on. Her reflection in the window caught her unawares. It was smiling at her. She put her hand in her pocket and felt the paper. It was smooth. A different softness from the lining of her coat. More earthy and real somehow.

The letter had arrived a few weeks before and Linda Parson had put it on the sideboard in her small kitchen. It was addressed to her. In large letters it stated, "Not to be opened before June 1st". She hadn't read it. She was curious of course but somehow didn't find it hard to resist. In an odd way she enjoyed the time before things happened and surely something would happen once she opened the letter. Also she had decided a long time ago that it was always better to do as one was told. Linda did not like trouble.

So she had dealt with the letter as she had been told to do. Every so often she would stop whatever she was doing. She would wipe her hands on her trousers and pick up the envelope. Gently turning it over to read the neat letters which laboriously spelt out her name and address. But she would not open it. Her mind of course would wander and wonder. June the 1st was her birthday but it didn't look like a birthday card. The envelope was brown and oblong. The handwriting wasn't familiar and anyway, apart from the monthly black printed bills, she wasn't used to getting much post.

She didn't open it but couldn't put it out of her mind. The postmark was Derby. She knew no-one there. Had never been to that part of the country though she did remember buying a train ticket to Derby for Jason. He was going to Alton Towers with friends. A birthday treat. But that was 14 years ago. Today Jason was serving time in Birmingham prison.

She thought about the letter in the day and she thought about it at night too. Once or twice or was it three times that week she got up in the middle of the night and made her way to the kitchen. Quietly so as not to wake up the neighbours downstairs. Sitting near the letter in the dark somehow brought her comfort. In a strange way also she was in charge of the letter. It was her choice to choose not to open it. And choice was not a word she used often.

Linda had always felt that life moved in ways over which she had little control. A black and white silent movie. She had sat there watching it helplessly. Paralysed with fear she'd witnessed her dad beat up her mum as a kid and later developed a technique for stepping outside her body as his hand resonated on her skin. In her twenties he thought she had found love but Michael didn't hang around to see their copper-haired baby grow. Her mum's death soon after that hit her heart into a sort of anxious stillness. Alone. She was alone. For years as tiredness brought her to bed in the evening and a sense of duty pulled her to work in the morning she felt she had no power over the way things were. She had to feed and care for her son. When he got involved with the bad boys there was nothing she could do. And she had resigned herself to what she thought was her fate as the judge pronounced the seven year sentence for Jason.

That was five years ago. After that she had filled her days with her job in the local supermarket and the household chores that needed doing. At night she relied on the regular programmes on TV. In an odd way she had enjoyed the quietness in that part of her life. She felt secure in the routine she had created for herself. She had more time to make friends. She had met them at work and later at her local bingo club where she enjoyed the occasional outing. Not close friends, but still. People whose company she enjoyed and who seemed to enjoy hers.

Things had changed at the end of the summer a little bit more than a year ago. One of her bingo friends had been made manageress of the local post office and had invited them all to celebrate at the Eagle. It was a warm Saturday night. They had sat outside drinking wine and chatting the time away. She was wearing a flowery dress that twirled when she walked. To this day she could remember the smell of the night too. The garden wall was covered in green interspersed with small clusters of pale yellow tubular flowers and the air was heavy with a heady scent. Honeysuckle Maria had said. Linda was having a good time. Her friends were laughing and she was laughing. Girlie chats. She was sitting at the end of the table and he had sat on the bench nearby. He started the conversation. Something to flatter her at first. The colour of her eyes and the sparkle of the stars. His

own eyes were narrow but very blue. Then he moved on
to other things. The pub and the bus routes. She enjoyed
the soft husk of his voice. He talked about food too and
the dogs at Belle Vue. He said he would take her there.
She had seen it on TV. She liked the place where his
arms met his wrists. The skin was taut. Underneath the
muscles and the bones. When he offered to take her back
home she realised her friends had gone.

Two months later he had moved out of the
flat he shared with his brother and moved in with her.
Things were not so bad at first. She had enjoyed the
coolness he brought into the bed at the end of his
nightshift. She liked her sleep to be broken by his desire.
However with time he had lost all inhibition and made
himself more forceful. His early gentleness had been
replaced by raw instinct. Meat. She had soon started to
feel like meat in his arms. He would take her and discard
her like some useless toy until the next night. Slowly
and perversely other aspects of her life became difficult.
Andy moaned about the slightest things and held her
responsible for anything and everything. Linda had been
brought up to accept the unacceptable. Somewhere
inside a little voice said she had made her own bed
and had to lie in it. So she passively submitted. Now
though the brown envelope vaguely reminded her of her
childhood. Of a long forgotten sense of hope.

The day before her birthday went quickly. She
went to work and when she came back he was watching
television. Football and snooker. That's how he spent
most days. Dinner was sausages and chips. She ate
nothing. She was not hungry. The letter. That was all she
could think of.

She had worked out where and when she would

do it. On the sofa at midnight. And a glass of white wine for when the moment came. He finally left for work at about 7.30 and she took his place in front of the small box. She would wind the hours away until midnight. The television was good at spinning time. Cookery. House buying. Traveling. Fiction. Television took her around the world. She could be in tens of people's shoes in the space of an evening.

When the red numbers by the side of her bed flashed 12 Linda turned off the television. She picked up the letter that had been resting on her lap since early on in the evening and tucked her feet under her. She slowly undid the flap of the envelope and carefully removed the letter that was inside. One sheet of school-lined paper neatly folded into three in its length. She unfolded the letter. And started reading.

Dear Mum,
I hope youre well.
Its' me. Jason.
Happy birthday.
I hope youre having a good day, with friends or something.

It was nice to see you awhile back. Busy and noisy with all them kids in the corner but nice. (Thanks' for getting me the chocolate and coke from the tuckshop.)
I've been going to these classes, learning to read and write. Again. The teecher lives in Derby so she sais she'll post the letter from home.

Your lovin son Jason

By the way sorry about evrything mum.

When she'd finished reading it Linda realized her bottom lip was sore. Her teeth had been biting into it. The glass of wine by the sofa was untouched. Her hands were shaking slightly and her face was burning. She felt her cheeks with the back of her left hand. They were wet.

She turned her head towards the door of the flat. The awful day when the police had turned up on her doorstep seemed like yesterday. There were two of them. A man and a woman standing there in their uniform. They had asked her to sit down and then had both sat facing her. The woman had done the talking. Jason had been caught with blood on his shirt. The blood belonged to a young man who was now in hospital. They talked of GBH. GBH with intent. There were witnesses.

The lawyer later explained what it all meant. GBH with intent. Grievous Bodily Harm. Jason had attacked someone and he had planned it. A pub fight turned nasty down a lane. What it also meant was 7 years behind bars. He was young but it wasn't the first time he had been caught fighting. And he was known to the police for stealing too. In fact the verdict was lenient. Because of his age the judge had said.

He was young. Slightly built. His skin sore and raw. Eyes that had stopped looking straight when his voice had broken. A truant who had never liked school. She had loved him as best as she could but it had not been enough.

He had grown a bit since. Still he looked so lost the last time she had seen him. Lost in the bright orange bib he and the other inmates had been given to wear.

But now this letter. Maybe all these years of caring and all that love had not been for nothing after

"What's that about an aunt, I never knew you had one… Come on girl where are you going?"

"Spain. I am going away for a month. "

"Away… Tonight?"

"No. Tomorrow morning."

"Why? Are you going with Andy?"

"No. Sort of getting away from him." Linda had never said much to anyone about Andy. She did not confide in people. Did not know how. Today was different.

"Can't say I blame you. And you going on your own? What did he say?"

"Yes on my own and he doesn't know yet… In fact if he comes around will you do me a favour and say you don't know where I've gone."

"What is it? Has something happened?"

"No, not really. But I think I've had enough. It's been a while. Things have not been right. And something came from Jason."

A customer was making his way towards her and then another one. She smiled and put each item through the scanner. Mechanically. Years of practice. Things at the till quietened down after a while and Maria asked,

"Something from your boy?"

"He sent me a card and it's a good card. He seems different. He seems to have changed. And if he can then so can I."

"What are you talking about Linda?"

"Changing things around in my life. I've been thinking of it for a while but never thought I could."

"You mean Andy?"

"Yes, things are not right and have not been for a while. Not sure why I put up with him really."

"He's not going to go easily though, is he?"

"Well I'm hoping that when I get back he'll have forgotten about me."

"Live in hope as my gran used to say."

"Yes, I'll have to see what happens."

Some people came along to go through the tills.

"And then what Linda?"

"Well I'll have to see. There's Jason."

"Jason! You don't really mean to take him back do you?"

"Yes. I am thinking about it."

"Won't it be lots of trouble? He's going to be a grown man you know with his own stuff going on?"

"I know but I should really give it a go. Also about Andy, I'm sure I don't want him around any more. No matter what happens."

That night when she got back the flat looked bare but nice. Uncluttered. She fell asleep quickly. Her flight was just before 6. In the very early hours of the morning she got up and ready. She looked around before closing the door behind her. She smiled to herself as she walked down the stairs to the taxi that was taking her to the station. In her bag along with the new shiny key was a letter that had been on the counter. Andy would try to come back. She was pleased she wasn't going to be there. He would go to his brother's. And hopefully when she got back he would leave her alone. His bright blue eyes would soon catch a new prey.

Once she had settled into her hotel room Linda explored the streets near the hotel. On that first day she didn't venture too far. She found a dress in a little boutique. A pink and blue dress. She liked what she saw in the mirror and bought it. As she opened her bag she saw the letter and smiled to herself.

A few days later Linda was sitting in a café on the beach. She was reading a book bought quickly in the airport. The title page looked good and it had nice reviews. She was reading. Not something she had done since leaving school. Oblivious to the downs and ups of her life her toes were searching the sand. She was not brown nor would she ever be but she glowed in the yellow light of the Spanish sun. Tomorrow and the day after and the day after were waiting to be written.

Marion *Lyme Regis*

*"Marion hadn't seen her
children play like this since
they were young. Back
then they'd play all the time.
It's why she'd had a large
family. She liked to watch her
children crawling over each
other like day old puppies in
a basket."*

Lucy Cavendish

Marion Lyme Regis
Lucy Cavendish

Marion sat on the bench above the beach and watched her three daughters as they played down below her. It was a typical British summer day, grey clouds scudding across the sky, interspersed with patches of blue. As soon as the sun shone out, Marion would feel the warmth infiltrating the cotton of her summer shirt and gently caressing her skin. These brief interludes made Marion feel hopeful. She had looked at the forecast before they'd left their home in South West London a few days ago and it had depicted rain clouds everywhere. She had then done what she always did. She'd packed for all eventualities, folding pac-a-macs back in to their tiny bags and, at the same time, slipping tubes of factor 30 in to all her children's bags.

They could pack for themselves now of course. They were that age. But Marion couldn't help herself from having a rummage through the night before they were about to leave. After all, what if they had forgotten something important? She'd done it for so long, checked on the knickers, the swimmers, the socks, the toothpaste, hairbrushes, toothbrushes. She really didn't think she could change the habit of a lifetime now.

It was a three-hour drive to Lyme Regis. As Marion had set off five days ago through the streets of East Sheen and out down the M3, she realised that no one else in the car was really aware of her at all. She was

161

their driver, the person who carried their bags, listened to them, paid for trips and fed them. No one had asked her why they were going to Lyme. No one had made any connection between the book that was peeking from her bag. That was why they were going down there, for Marion to see where *The French Lieutenant's Woman* was set. It meant so much to her but obviously so little to anyone else. Marion realised that she had become almost invisible to her family. She existed now merely to provide the members of it with food, shelter, clean clothes and money when they needed things. The rest of the time Marion believed they didn't really notice her.

This didn't come as a shock. The thought had been brewing in her mind for some time. The girls' lives, that were once so intrinsically linked to her own, had now become about everything but her. Whereas once she would have been down there with them on the beach – laughing with them as they ran away from the sea, wrapping their cold salt-licked bodies up in the endless warm towels she'd have lugged down with her – her daughters now moved almost as a cabal, a cabal she wasn't included in. They spent their lives watching You Tube, texting friends, messing about on Facebook, disappearing off to parties with people she barely knew. Occasionally, just occasionally, they'd say, "how are you Mum?" but when she'd open her mouth to speak, they'd wander off or start on a new topic of conversation with one or other of their sisters.

As for her son Joss, he spent most of his time in his room, refusing to come out and, on the odd occasion when he did – usually to demand food – he'd merely grunt.

It wasn't raining though, thank God. When

Marion looked at the sky, she felt that they'd be OK, that maybe the summer rain jackets she'd made her daughters come out in were superfluous. They had come down to the breakfast this morning wearing their usual uniform of leggings, shorts over the top, low-cut tee-shirts and lots of jewellery. They had, on this sixth morning at the Cobb Inn, looked appalled by what was yet again on offer; fried eggs, bacon, bread, sausage, tomato. They had stared at the other guests of the hotel who nodded silently to the Polish waitress when she brought them the mounds of fat-covered food piled high on plates.

"I CAN'T EAT THAT!" hissed Livia, her youngest daughter, now 14, as her own plate, complete with a steaming mushroom, was put down in front of her. "I keep telling you that Mum. Every day I've asked you to get me something else. Don't they have any yoghurt or something?"

Mel, her middle daughter two years older, pulled a face. "You're gonna get fat if you eat all that Livs," she said. "You're going to look like Big Fat Sally in 8c."

"NO I'M BLOODY NOT!" yelled back Livia, pushing the plate away. "You're going to get fat coz you've ordered baked beans. Baked beans, good for the heart. The more you eat, the more you.."

"Livia!" Marion had interrupted. "Eat your breakfast and stop being silly and stop moaning. Of course I asked for a sheep's yoghurt but this is Lyme, not London."

Then she had looked at Joss and Imo, her two eldest, 17 and 19 respectively. Imo was reading a book as per usual and Joss was glowering at the blank television that was pushed to the back of the room.

"I thought we'd be able to watch it," he said, his voice tight with anger. "That television doesn't work and it's the final tonight and Mum, you said…"
Marion had sighed then.

"We will," she said. "We'll find a pub. We'll…"
Imo has pursed her lips primly. She pushed her glasses up her nose a little bit.

"Mum," she said carefully. "I understand that football is important to Joss but I, for one, do not want to spend our last night here in a pub watching the World Cup final. I totally get that Joss wants to but..well..I don't."

"That's OK," said Marion absent-mindedly watching the couple next to her who, having fought their way silently through two eggs and accompanying sausages, were now sitting staring in to space. Marion wished Pete had been able to come but he'd told her work couldn't spare him. They wouldn't have sat in silence. They would have had things to talk about – the weather, the food, the scenery. This is how they had spent all these married years of their life, just gently chatting the time away. But Pete had given her the same response as usual.

"Sorry, Love," he'd said ruefully. "If I'd had more notice."

Marion had decided to come to Lyme Regis almost on the spur of the moment. She very rarely did anything at short notice, especially not with four children. But she had decided that the children's end of term exams were over, and the summer crowds would not have gathered yet and so maybe it was a good time to go. She had no idea when they would all be in the same place at the same time again so, in an instant, she decided to get all the children together and set off. But then there'd been the threat of rain and the non-working television at the rather run-down bed and breakfast she had found such a cheap deal at and she'd begun to wonder if it had been a good idea at all. They were supposed to be bonding, hanging out, existing in each other's space but, so far, all they'd been were tensions and rows. She knew her children were at that age, but the constant griping at each other and the bleeping of endless text messages from friends and the unspoken but definitely there sense she had that somehow it was all her fault was beginning to get her down. She started every day looking at the sea rolling in and rolling out and she thought that she was like the froth on the top of one of those huge dark waves being carried along and that there was nothing she could do to stop it.

Not that her daughters seemed to have noticed. Her dark mood totally passed them by. As the day began to warm up, they had taken off their shorts, peeled their leggings up to reveal white legs that hadn't seen the sun for an age. They'd tied their cagoules round their waists and were now staring at their feet busily looking for crabs. Marion could hear their shrieks above the sound of the sea crashing in and out.

"There's one under there. There is, really!" yelled Livia, almost dancing on the spot with glee.

"No there's bloody not," Mel shouted back, peering down towards the rocks and squinting.

"Yes there is!" said Livia insistently. "I can see its claws! I really can. It's huge! It's going to bite me!"

"No it's bloody not!" yelled Mel. "Coz there's not one there. You've made it up."

"I have not!"

"Oh yes you bloody have."

Marion watched at Imo stood up straight.

"Maybe I can see it," she said, bending back down again to peer at the rocks and adjusting her glasses so they didn't fall off. That was typical of Imo, thought Marion. She was always the peacemaker; fair, studious, quiet. Sometimes Marion would find herself watching her children and wondering who they were. Livia she felt she knew. There was an energy in Livia that struck a beat in Marion's heart every time she saw her. She could deny Livia nothing. She had tried but there was something about her – was it her physical beauty perhaps, with her long limbs, blonde hair, green eyes, a goddess? – that made Marion almost euphoric every time she saw her.

Mel was the sporty one. Marion had never been sporty so she could marvel at the way Mel managed to manipulate her body to run faster, jump higher, hit balls with bats with greater accuracy than Marion could ever have hoped for.

But Imo was impenetrable. She had always been like that. As a baby, Imo would lie there with her wide blue eyes and slightly naturally-pursed mouth and a solemn look that made Marion squirm. It was as if Imo knew everything about Marion and it made Marion feel terribly exposed. She'd always felt that, when she talked to Imo, she somehow wasn't being herself, that she was putting on pretence to stop that penetrating gaze.

"That baby's old before her years," everyone would say to her and Marion would give a little forced smile and say, "yes isn't she?" Pete, oddly enough, tended to feel most at home with Imo. It quite freaked her out, this large family of hers.

Marion sighed. She wondered if this was the

last time she'd see her daughters together quite like this. Soon Imo would be off to study psychology and their family would have lost the first member from its nest.

Marion hadn't seen her children play like this since they were young. Back then they'd play all the time. It's why she'd had a large family. She liked to watch her children crawling over each other like day old puppies in a basket. On holidays it was the same but more so, no concern for school time, homework, activities. There'd be sandcastles on the beach on family holidays in Devon, Cornwall, the Scilly Isles, hot chips, ice cream cornets, battered fish, buckets, and spades. There'd be cold winds, slashing rain and then occasionally, days like today where the sun would burn out eventually and by midday she'd be slathering on sun lotion and putting up umbrellas and then, if she was lucky, sinking back and watching the children as they slithered around in the sand like snakes. Not that she ever had much time for herself. She was always packing up the beach bags full of towels, swimsuits, changes of clothes, water, sun tan lotion. Then, when she wasn't packing and unpacking the beach bag, she was making sandcastles, digging out moats, finding shells to make patterns on the sand with.

There were too many dull days though, spent at rain-soaked amusement parks, sodden fun fairs, indoor play centres with ball parks that smelled of stale urine and day-old food. Marion would have liked to have gone further afield. She wouldn't have minded trying Brittany maybe, introduced the children to snails, frogs legs and fruits de mer, but Pete wouldn't hear of it.

"There's too many of us," he'd say. "We can't afford the Continent."

Marion looked at the girls again. They were

167

skimming stones on the waves now and shrieking with laughter. It made her smile. She glanced to her left and saw Joss sitting on a rock, shoulders hunched, clad in an anorak, hood up.

"It's warm Joss," Marion called out to him. He looked up and glowered at her and then turned back towards the beach. He started to throw stones down on to the shingle below him.

He was in a bad mood, Marion could tell. She usually felt sympathetic towards him. She knew it couldn't have ever been that easy to be sandwiched between these girls. She and Pete had been convinced, after they'd had him, that they'd be due another boy. With each ensuing pregnancy, they were sure there would be another but the two girls followed and Joss had to spend a childhood surrounded by Barbie dolls and nail varnish. This didn't seem to bother him. He generally treated the dolls and other girlish paraphernalia with good humour and rarely chopped off the hair of the Barbie's and only once actually gouged out some eyes. After he hit 13 though, he retreated in to his bedroom, turned on his X-Box and rarely came out.

Pete worried about Joss more than anyone else in the family, Marion thought. He often said how distant he felt from his son. Marion would nod and be sympathetic and yet, in all honestly, she found herself feeling at ease with Joss. His mood swings never really concerned her. She just saw it as part and parcel of his growing up and, in many ways, his silent adolescence was easier to deal with than the girls' endless anxieties.

But, today, his bad mood irked her. Why did Joss have to complain so much on this particular holiday?

Over the last few days he'd gone on and on

about the lack of people to play with, the fact the television didn't work, the horrible food, the paucity of biscuits in the room, the heat, the cold but, mostly, that he was missing the end of the World Cup.

It had started on the way down in the car when he droned on and on about it.

"Do they have a television in the hotel?" he'd eventually asked.

"Of course they do, Dummy," Mel had replied. "We're going to Lyme Regis, not Calcutta."

"Yeah but I wanted to watch it with my mates."

"What mates? You don't have any. You just sit in your room and talk to people on line."

"They're pretend mates aren't they?" said Livia chipping in.

"No they're not. They're…"

His complaints were drowned out by a cacophony of noise as Mel's boyfriend texted her.

"Ooh," said Livia. "He says he "hearts" you." Mel made an L sign and showed it to her sister.

"I am not a loser!" yelled Livia in response. "Imo, am I a loser?"

"No, you're a lezzer," cut in Mel before Imo could answer.

"What do you mean I'm a bloody lezzer."

"I saw your Facebook page. You told that Laura friend of yours that you loved her."

"She's my bloody friend. You can have a friend who's a girl. That doesn't make you a lezzer."

"Yes it does. You're a dyke, that's what you are."

"Imo," said Livia. "Please. Help."

"What?" said Imo.

"I'm not a dyke am I? Just coz I love Laura?"

169

"No," said Imo, staring out of the car window. "You're not a dyke and, anyway, it's a very insulting term and Mel should know better than to use that word." She looked at her sister. "Don't you know better than that?"

"She said lezzer!" said Mel, pointing at Livia. "I mean, that's a bloody insulting word too isn't it?" Imo sighed.

"Yes. Grow up, both of you."

Joss then made an L sign at Mel.

"A loser? Am I a bloody loser?"

"Yes," said Joss glowering. "You're all bloody losers."

Marion sighed in frustration and thought about how, one night, about a month ago, when they were in the sitting room one evening, him reading his newspaper, her reading her book, she'd told Pete how she really felt.

"I'm not happy," she'd said. He'd looked at her. He seemed surprised.

"Why love?" he'd said.

"I think I've got empty nest syndrome," she said. "Where's this come from?"

"I don't know. I've just been thinking about it really. I look at the children and I think how much I've loved them and how used I am to looking after them. I worry what I'm going to do without them and…"

"But they haven't left yet!" he'd replied. "And you'll have me."

"I know," she'd said trying hard not to sound sad. "But I don't know what to do with myself. I've been a mother for so long and now…now…I don't exist for them." She'd then felt embarrassed, as if she had overstepped some shadowy boundary that, previously, she hadn't noticed existed. She hurriedly opened the pages of the book she was reading.

"I don't know who I am anymore," she said to him, staring at the words on the pages and willing herself not to cry. Her husband patted her arm. Then he looked at the book. *The French Lieutenant's Woman.*

"What would she say?" he'd said.

It had made Marion blush. In truth, she knew it was getting a bit obsessive. She'd signed up for a local English Literature adult education evening class to give herself something to do. She'd seen the advert in a local newspaper and, in a rare moment of sudden decisiveness, called up and enrolled on the course. She then spent the next few weeks getting herself in to a state about it. Why on earth was she doing this? Then she'd tell herself it was good for her to try something new, expand her brain. Pete was always telling her she needed to get out more, find something for herself. So she'd steeled herself to walk through the door that first evening. She'd felt nervous but the young male teacher was welcoming and the other "students" were all about her age so soon she'd relaxed in to it. She had worried that she would seem, well, very un-literary as her ability to sit down and read a book had rapidly diminished since she'd had the children. She'd romped through Austen, Hardy, the occasional Dickens and, when she wanted a real secret treat, had let herself read a Jilly Cooper. But, since the children, it had tended to be magazines and crosswords.

The French Lieutenant's Woman by John Fowles was the first book they were studying in the class and she had gradually become entranced by it. It wasn't just the novelty of it all – having the time to read, getting her brain to creak in to gear again. It wasn't just the thought that this was something she was doing for herself, although that idea had popped in to her head, making her feel slightly selfish. At first she assumed it might be because of the secret private enjoyment she felt when she sat and opened the book. In fact, the book had really got to her. From the moment she began reading it, she was transported back to a time she hadn't thought about since she'd put down her Dickens all those years ago. It seemed masterful to her, the depiction of Lyme Regis with its layers of society tucked away amongst the geography of the place; the hills, the woods, the sea and, most importantly, the Cobb with the stormy waves that battered it day by day. She could see it in her mind and was desperate to go there to find out if her imagination had seen it correctly. The more they studied it in class, the more she began to feel the main character, Sarah Woodruff, being peeled away.

Marion would avidly read passages about how the socially-rejected former governess would stare out to sea, standing at the end of the Cobb, waiting for the married French lover she knew would never return. For a long time Marion wrestled with this. In every page, there was rejection, trickery, difficulties. Why would Sarah stand there waiting for someone who would never return? Why would she so willingly, somewhat helplessly, put herself in a situation that made her a social outcast? It was as if she wanted it to rile people, to get under their skin and then sometimes it was as if she couldn't help it, that she had been so possessed by a fearful love that she was driven to expose herself in such a terrible fashion.

Marion would then find herself staring out of her own garden window, desperate for something to happen to her. How amazing Sarah Woodruff was. How

strong-willed! The book seemed so passionate, so full
of longing and anxiety and, as the it went on, Marion
began to see and admire Sarah Woodruff a unique
woman. She would sit in class and try hard not to close
her eyes, imagining the thrill of passion between Sarah
and Charles, the cat and mouse nature of their courtship,
how daring and yet frustrating Sarah Woodruff could
be. Her teacher had told her there could be many
readings of Sarah Woodruff – elusive, wilful, deliberately
enigmatic, manipulative even but, for Marion, she was
wonderfully complex, deeply romantic and verging on
true and real emancipation. Marion took a deep breath
in. She looked at the children. They were still turning
stones over. She only had a few chapters left and her aim
was to finish the book by the end of the day. She checked
her watch. She didn't have much time. She had to find
that pub for Joss. Maybe it would be good for all of them
to do something together, although she wasn't sure if a
football match was precisely what the girls had in mind.

She had just taken the book out of her bag,
feeling the thrill of anticipation, when a woman
appeared from behind her and sat down on the seat
next to her. Marion hadn't noticed her approaching at
all, barely heard any movement of feet on the dry grass
behind her yet, there she was, a woman, seated next to
Marion. She looked at her as surreptitiously as possible.
The woman seemed younger than her and had a very
pale, heart-shaped face. She was wearing a long dress
and Marion was struck how translucent her skin was
on her thin arms. She had something, a long piece of
material draped over her right arm. Marion couldn't tell.
She thought maybe it was a cape but no one wore capes
these days. Perhaps it was a form of raincoat, Marion

thought. Like her, this woman was not going to take chances with the weather.

But right now, in the sun, the woman's shoulders were reddening slightly. For a second, Marion thought she ought to offer her some protective lotion then she mentally checked herself. She was being a mother. The woman sitting next to her was a grown up, not one of her children. Just as she was about to look away, feeling embarrassed at the amount she was staring at the woman, the woman turned to her and smiled.

"Is this your first time to Lyme?" she asked her. She spoke with a strong West Country burr, the like of which Marion had never really heard outside dramatisations of plays she'd listen to on Radio 4 some afternoons.

Marion nodded.

"Have you enjoyed yourself?" the woman asked.

"Absolutely," Marion said. "We've had a great time and…unfortunately, it's our last day. We've had a lovely time though. Really lovely."

The woman didn't say anything. She just stared out towards the sea.

"The weather's been OK really," continued Marion, suddenly feeling the need to continue the conversation. "It's beautiful to be by the sea when the sun is shining, so rare in England…" Marion tailed off. Why was she saying all this stuff to a woman she didn't know?

But the woman looked at her and smiled. With her green eyes and blonde hair, Marion was a bit taken back. She was almost what Livia might be when she was grown up.

"So, you've been down to the Cobb?" asked the

woman.

"Yes. It's amazing. I don't think I've ever seen anything like it. I've watched it so much, the sea crashing down on to the stones when the wind is up. It's so dramatic."

The woman gave a lingering look towards the Cobb.

"It's a wonderful place," she said, "and it can be very dramatic. I've been watching it for a long time too. Maybe too long…"

"Do you live here?" Marion asked her. "You must do if you know the Cobb so well."

"Kind of," said the woman vaguely. "I used to live here. Now I've…well, I've moved on." Then she glanced at Marion and her eyes flickered to the book on Marion's lap. She gave an involuntary gasp.

"You are reading that?" she said quickly. "That book? It's the one you're reading?"

"Yes," said Marion blushing slightly. "That's why we've come here. I've been studying it in my English literature classes. I think the book paints Lyme Regis as being such a beautiful place with the cliffs and the woods. It's such a romantic story so I decided to come here with my children, to see where the action took place as it were."

"So you like the book?" the woman said.

"I love it," said Marion enthusiastically. And then, spurred on by a strange sense of longing in the woman's eyes, she felt inspired to continue.

"It's about this woman, Sarah Woodruff. She lives by…by her emotions really. She is enigmatic and wilful and…I have become very involved in it."

"Have you?"

"Yes! I can't put it down. It's like being

transported in to another world. The woman, Sarah Woodruff, is totally at odds with the society she lives in and she doesn't care. She really doesn't care!"

"Is that true?" said the woman. "That this Sarah Woodruff doesn't care? Does that make her free? Maybe she has no ties, or no ties that matter enough to her. How interesting." The woman looked away. Marion felt oddly cold all of a sudden. But the woman then turned back to her and said, "do you know why that is? Her need for freedom?"

"Yes," said Marion determinedly, feeling a need to explain herself although she wasn't sure why. "She's everything I am not. That is what releases her. She is a proper person. A real person. No one would feel as passionately about me as everyone does about Sarah. She took decisions that were very hard to take in that day and age. She chose love and abandonment above and beyond what society demanded of her. She took the rules and broke them."

"And you find this admirable?"

"I find it entrancing, yes. I find it life-affirming. It makes me believe maybe we should all be a bit more carefree in our lives."

"Or selfish. Could you see this Sarah Woodruff as being selfish?"

"I don't know. I just think she took hard decisions and made them for herself, not others. I need to make some hard decisions although I'm not sure what about. Something is missing in my life, although I don't know what it is. I am yearning for something but.."

The woman leaned forward. "But what?" she said urgently. "What is it? We all yearn, oh how we yearn so what is it you yearn for?"

Marion looked down at the beach towards her children. The woman followed her gaze.

"My children don't seem to realize or care that I exists. My husband tries his best but…we barely see each other. He works hard. He has always work hard yet we never have any money. I want more. I want to risk things. I want to holiday abroad. I want to eat strange food. I want people to listen to me, to be moved by me. Even the people who don't approve of Sarah have feelings about her." Marion looked down quickly to the ground. Why on earth was she telling the woman this? But there was something about her…

"No one feels anything about me," she said suddenly, twisting her wedding ring round on her finger. "I've become invisible you see, utterly invisible and it makes me want to…I don't know, run away, change something, find myself in the way Sarah is finding herself."

The woman sat back on the bench and looked at her thoughtfully.

"Have you got to the end of the book yet?" she said.

Marion shook her head.

The woman quickly put her hand on Marion's. Her skin felt oddly cold and clammy.

"Don't finish it," she said. "There are so many endings to this story. What can happen to this woman that is good? Maybe she marries Charles and lives happily ever after, although cloaked in shame of course in her own way for she has taken a man betrothed to another.."

"But this is precisely what I am talking about!" said Marion. "I know she will end up somewhere with

177

Charles in some seaside town in a b and b probably not
that dissimilar from where we are staying. But what guts
to do that! What passion!"

"Yes, but what about sacrifice? Sarah never truly
learns the meaning of that day-to-day sacrifice. Maybe
Charles marries his fiancée and is unhappy and spends
his life tracking Sarah down. Maybe she has a child she
never tells him about."

"All these maybes!" says Marion, almost
shouting.

"Yes, and you don't want those maybes. You are
in your own story, not that of Sarah Woodruff. Let Sarah
continue in your mind as a wonderful person who has
spirit. Don't read on. Be happy with where you are." As
she said this, the young woman looked momentarily sad.
"Maybe you will learn from her, from her triumphs and
mistakes."

"I don't understand," said Marion, feeling
strangely deflated.

"I fear it will not come good for her. It never
does. Surely you know that? Don't you know that? Oh
you do! Women like that never really find happiness.
They make, how can I say? The wrong decisions.
They are too wilful, too full of their own private and
destructive passions. Oh I think this Sarah Woodruff
is probably a very selfish woman who listens to no one.
Sometimes, it is the marriage and children that should
be honoured. I fear this Sarah will never know that and
it will be of great sadness to her. Look to that Marion.
Think of that. Your children, your husband, wonderful,
true miraculous things. Think of that Marion. Think of
that…"

Marion looked down at her daughters. She saw that Joss

had joined them down on the beach and that they were trying to bury him under a mound of pebbles. Marion saw, for a second, and with relieved surprise, that Joss was smiling.

She turned to the woman to tell her that she was right, that her children and her husband meant everything and that she really knew that deep down in her heart, but the woman had gone. Marion stood up and looked around her. For a moment, she was puzzled. How could the woman have disappeared from sight that quickly? She craned her neck and turned this way and that, but the woman really had gone. She sat down again, feeling puzzled.

Then she sighed, picked up her book with a mild sense of disappointment. She had enjoyed talking. It had helped. She would have liked to have talked on further but, right now, she was not going to get the book she finished and, judging by the cheer she heard ricocheting round the cliffs above her, she'd lost all track of time and the match was about to begin. She quickly gathered her things up and walked down to the beach to her children.

"Hi Mum!" said Livia when she saw her. "We've been having such a great time. What have you been up to?"

The children turned to look at her, their faces flushed and flecked with salt.

"I met a woman," said Marion. "She knew the book I'm reading so we got to chatting."

"What woman?" said Mel? "I didn't see you with anyone."

"Well, she wasn't there for long. Just for the last ten minutes or so. Maybe you've been busy playing."

"No," said Imo thoughtfully. "I've been watching

you and no one else was with you."

"Really?" said Marion. "But there was someone there. She was tall and fair. She looked oddly like you Livia."

"Nope, we saw no one" said Livia, bending down to skim a stone. It bounced six times across the waves.

"A sixer!" she yelled. "Bet no one can beat that!"

"Mum, there really wasn't anyone there," said Imo. "I mean you've been sitting there for an age and no one's been anywhere near you."

"How do you know that?"

"You've been talking to yourself Mum," said Joss. "I've been bloody waving at you, trying to get your attention, and you've just been staring in to space rabbiting on to yourself."

"I have not!" said Marion. "Why on earth would I do that?"

"I don't care," said Joss. "We need to go to a pub and watch the match and we need to go right now, mad woman."

"I am not mad Josh."

"Well, we were all looking at you coz you were gabbling away to yourself. That's what mad people do isn't it?"

Marion stared at him then she looked back up to the bench and shivered.

"But there was a woman there," she said. "How could you not have seen her? She was wearing a long dress and her shoulders were burning in the sun and…I don't really understand."

"I'm hungry Mum," said Mel, picking up her jumper. "Let's go and find some food eh?"

She went to move up the beach, Livia following her.

"Bout bloody time," said Joss as he sloped off after them.

Marion took one last glance at the bench. The she turned to Imo.

"Mum?" said Imo questioningly beginning to follow her siblings. "You coming?"

"Yes," said Marion, picking up her bag. "Of course. I'm paying aren't I?"

Then, tucking the book firmly back in to her bag, she walked up the beach, following her children rather than leading as before.

10

Helen *Archmont Terrace*

"This young woman's loneliness was different to Helen's, but Helen sensed that it ran equally deep. It was strange, this world of the single feminine spirit; it was one she hadn't contemplated before, its existence, its prevalence."

Miranda Glover

Helen Archmont Terrace
Miranda Glover

There were four cottages in Archmont Terrace. Each had a wooden latch gate to the front, flanked by traditional, low brick and flint front garden walls that separated them from one another and from the village high street. All four had smooth, paved paths, as deep-set as gravestones, polished smooth by eight generations of boots and shoes, of more than 130 seasons; of snow and ice and wind and rain and drought and frost, of damp and dry. To all intents and purposes, they were your traditional two up, two down workmen's cottages, originally built for farmhands on the local country estate. They all had an outdoor loo block now used to store tools or logs, and a linear washing line half way up their long, narrow back gardens, whose winding paths led to compost heaps, a shanty town of garden sheds and greenhouses and back gates, which in turn led out onto one of the lanes that ran like a warren through the village, between the houses. The lanes were too narrow for cars, but wide enough for bicycles and babies' buggies, for walkers and joggers, for foxes and badgers and for lovers' embraces on moonless nights.

Now two of the four cottages had mansard extensions in their attics, which from the front gave them the appearance of an extra set of hooded eyes above the smaller windows on the first floor. They belittled the views from the lower floors, with their superior, high

185

vantage points. From the top of these two cottages you could see the comings and goings of the locals along the village high street: walking their dogs, ferrying their children to the primary school, riding their horses past. Look right and you could see the village shop-cum-post-office, too and to the left straight into the car park adjoining The Walnut Tree pub. This was still a village, with an active community and a real sense of itself; not one of those villages that had lost its heartbeat the locals would tell you with mounting pride, but one where the pulse was still well and truly alive. A village where real people lived, a village where things happened.

From the mansards at the back, you could also see above the old stonewalls onto the lane and into the meadows beyond, and on across the glorious, rolling Berkshire Downs. If you craned your neck left you could also see the brick and flint church with its elegant spire and its mournful bell, hanging heavily in its tower. When the doors were pulled back for a service, you could even see the backs of the congregation's heads and the altar with its weekly-changing floral arrangement. You couldn't quite see the vicar, but you could see the pulpit where he stood and the swishing hems of his heavy, purple and white robes.

Because Archmont Terrace was set back from the street slightly, the cottages had a sense of privacy about them; they were diminutive and unassuming compared to some of the larger houses around. If you weren't thinking about it, you could almost forget that they were there. Three of them had low-maintenance, blowsy wild flower cottage gardens to the front, which almost camouflaged them completely from passers-by. By way of contrast, the fourth, or indeed, the first, Number

One, "Magnolia Cottage," had a recently nurtured, immaculate arrangement of neat beds flourishing with carnations, sweet peas, roses and a rare, ornamental magnolia tree at its centre, surrounded by a neatly cut, daisy-speckled lawn. It had a stone statue, too, the kind you get from garden centres, of a naked female ballet dancer, balancing on one toe, her second leg extended backwards, slightly raised, elegant, artistic. This front garden was distinctly feminine and, compared to the other gardens, a little sophisticated. The statue had raised a few eyebrows for its immodesty when the new owner first placed it there, but that was nearly three years ago now and people had got used to it, as they do to most things in the end.

It was Helen Llewellyn who lived at Number One. A regular listener to Radio Four's Gardeners' Question Time. In the year after she arrived, she'd thrown all her emotional energy into the creation of a perfect oasis for herself and her cat, Poncho. She had finally peeled herself away from her husband, Jack, at sixty-five years old. Her decision had rocked the family, like a tsunami crashing onto their shore, shattering all semblance of normality. It had apparently eroded the foundations that her two children, Jane and Michael said they had "believed in" too - or so they had told her, a touch scornfully, at the time.

"You'll all get over it," Helen had told them. "For God's sake, you're both in your thirties now, don't tell me we're still your bedrocks."

Her outburst had met with a shocked silence from both children, who had looked pitifully over at their father, sitting in his armchair for their 'joint announcement' - which is what Helen had wanted. In response he had simply shrugged his shoulders towards the children and raised his eyes skyward. Helen knew what they were all thinking: that it was outrageous, unspeakable, for her to behave like this. She could almost read their minds; she's gone completely bonkers, they thought.

But Helen hadn't gone bonkers at all. In fact, she felt more sane than she had done for years. With their reaction she had felt her defiance mount, and a previously unknown, stirring strength of certitude rising inside her too. It wasn't up to her anymore, to hold them all together. She had broken free. They would all have to do it for themselves from now on. She felt a huge weight lifting from her shoulders, the weight of responsibility. To her surprise, she also found that her years of smouldering loathing for her husband and his mini-minded ways evaporated too, and in place of these high emotions she simply felt a bit sad and sorry, that she had waited so long, that he would have to learn to cope on his own at this late stage. It would in many ways have been kinder to have done it a long time before.

She tried to feel guilty about her decision, but she couldn't quite convince herself that she was wholly culpable. He had always been a selfish man, self-obsessed and a little bit pompous; never contrite, never truly generous, a bad listener. She had suffered him for all of these years out of a sense of duty, for the sake of the children, for the status quo, she supposed. When she looked at him now, he seemed an awful lot older than her too, with his aches and his pains, his tedious somnolence in the afternoons. She was "sprightly and lithe at sixty-five" as one of her friends had written on her birthday card; she had dealt well with the menopause, was past the HRT and all that now, and felt she had a bright, long future ahead of her. She wasn't at all bothered about finding a new relationship; in fact she fast discovered that she loved being alone. It felt so refreshing, not to have to share any more. Not to have to give. To be able to go to bed every night with a good book and a cup of tea at nine, without even having bothered with supper, and Poncho curled up purring at the foot of the bed, for company, Radio Four on, or, now she knew how, a Podcast of the previous week's Gardeners' Question Time if she'd missed the last live recording. Life was great - or kind of. Three years on and the garden was perfect and her life was tranquil, but although she wouldn't confess to it to Jane or Michael, there was something nagging at her; something hard to pin down. A little gap, that seemed to be widening. She had located it to a space between her rib cage and her heart. It was hard to define quite what it was because it was numb, or blank, or a vacuum, or maybe even a hole. She wasn't quite sure how else to describe it.

Helen tried the church, to fill the gap. The psalms and hymns and scent of fresh flowers all perfumed her spirits for the moments that she was there; but by the time she got home again she found that the scent had already faded, its impact diminished to nothing, and she couldn't remember a word of the sermon, or its meaning either, without really trying to cast her mind back. During the service she felt as if she had been lifted out of herself, become adrift at sea, swayed with the waves, backwards and forwards, as if in a meditation, or in the arms of someone singing her a lullaby. She wondered if that was because of the vicar, rather than the content of his words. He was old-fashioned, which felt comfortable. He didn't call his parishioners by their first names unless they asked him too, (she was still Mrs Llewellyn to him, even after two years of regular attendance), and he didn't hold your hand for too long when he welcomed you to a service. He didn't mind if you wanted communion but weren't confirmed and he had a lilting voice that allowed you to float with his words until they became abstract, mingled with your sub-conscious, your innermost spirit. Maybe that was what it was; finding God. Helen wasn't sure.

"Funny thing you should remember, when you're painting in windows," she explained to her grandson, Tommy, one spring afternoon as they sat together on low wooden stools in the pretty, flower-filled back garden of Magnolia Cottage. "When you look at them during the day, they always appear black and it is almost impossible to see what's happening inside."

Tommy dipped the tip of his field brush into his pot of water, wiped it on the kitchen roll his granny had brought out with them from the kitchen, and then dipped it into the black tablet of watercolour. He pointed the tip of the brush at each of the windows he had drawn into his picture of the four houses in turn and allowed the colour to spread into the squares, as she had advised. Then he looked up at her and grinned. Helen smiled back, delighted. Her grandson appeared to share her observant eye, her artistic bent.

"The time you can observe the interior of a room is at dusk, when lights are on but the curtains are not yet closed," she added, as if to herself, as she drew her sable across the skyline of her watercolour paper and allowed it to spread, creating a soft, blue, billowing sky above her own interpretation of the row of terraces.

Being alone afforded one a more observing eye, it was true. Helen had found this on moving into this sleepy little community. Her daughter lived at the other end of the village and when she had left Jack, Helen had agreed to move closer to Jane. Often, throughout that third spring and summer, early in the evening, she would wander out of the back garden and along the winding lanes, to pay her daughter a visit. Callum, Jane's husband was regularly late home from work. It was the price they paid, for this country life, the distance from the city of London to West Berkshire was at least an hour and a half, door to door. It meant that during the week, her daughter was often alone with the children. This had proved a great bonus to Helen, giving a punctuation mark to the end of her day. Once she'd done in the garden, she often pottered around there and helped her daughter put them to bed. And then they'd have a small glass of Sauvignon together before she headed back home, slightly drowsy but content. That was when she got to look inside other people's houses; at that moment between night and day, when curtains aren't closed yet, but the lights have gone on.

One of the houses that she passed was the vicarage. The first time it happened was quite by accident; that she saw him and found herself pausing, absorbed. The vicar was a similar age to Helen, a widower who lived alone in the large, rambling old rectory. She'd heard it said that when he finally retired, or died, that the Church of England wanted to reclaim and sell the house; that it was too large and grandiose for its purpose these days, that it would fetch more than a million pounds on the commercial market. The topic, whenever raised, would send a shiver of irritation amongst its faithful as they sat in their pews, for the proceeds would not be returned to the village, but into the centralised coffers of the diocese.

What Helen saw that first evening as she stood in the lane, was a simple man, sitting at a large desk in the vicarage study, pouring over his papers, a single desk lamp switched on, the rest of the house in darkness. There was nothing particularly significant in this, but for the modesty, the quiet commitment to his faith, to God's work, that touched her. And his solitude too. She wondered suddenly, if, like her, he was ever lonely or if his faith negated the need for more intimate human, rather than spiritual contact. After a moment, Helen moved on, aware that her observation was intrusive, invasive. She would hate for him to look round, to see her standing there in the dusk alone.

But the next evening, when she went to visit Jane again, she found herself anticipating her return home up the lanes, before she had even drained her glass. When she passed the vicarage she tried to stop herself from glancing sideways, but found that her eyes drawn to the study window, where, as before, she found him sitting, concentrating on his papers.

On the evenings when Jane didn't visit Sarah, she now found herself restless by seven o'clock, desiring a moment of fresh air, a moment outside of the cocoon she had created for herself and Poncho. She would stand at her mansard window and watch the quiet high street, observe people coming and going to the pub, or taking their dogs for an evening walk and she would want to get outside. She would like to wander for a moment along the lanes. She would like to see him, sitting there, just for a moment. His presence felt reassuring. She couldn't explain why. And out she'd go, a touch furtively, without an errand or excuse. She'd glance back at the row of terraces, as she unlatched the back gate, to see if anyone noticed her evening-time ramblings. But there never seemed to be anyone home, or if there were, the curtains at this time appeared generally to be closed. No one was bothered by her movements; there was, she realised, no one to care.

The other terraces, curiously, were all now owned by single women too; one widower in her late seventies, one woman in her mid-fifties whose husband had upped and left her with their two teenage daughters, because "he'd had enough of all these females in one place".

Or so she'd heard. The third house was owned by a hard-working female lawyer in her early thirties, who seemed to spend most of the week in her London Chambers, before returning home for weekends alone, reading romantic fiction in the garden, or on the phone to her girlfriends. This young woman's loneliness was different to Helen's, but Helen sensed that it ran equally deep. It was strange, this world of the single feminine spirit; it was one she hadn't contemplated before, its existence, its prevalence. She could do it, this singularity, but she began to realise that what she felt in that gap between her ribcage and her heart was a certain despair, at having to. She also knew that she had made the choice for herself, that she hadn't needed to find herself, at sixty-eight alone. Regardless, when she thought of Jack, already bedded in with a new girlfriend he had met on the Internet, she didn't feel a moment's remorse.

Helen began to go to the Wednesday evensong service, as well as regular Sunday morning communion.

The vicar appeared increasingly delighted to see her, and if she wasn't mistaken, his tone seemed warmer towards her than to his other regular churchgoers. She noticed that he had incredibly deep-set eyes, and that when they looked at you, they seemed to see further than the surface of your expression, that they seemed to communicate more so with what lay within. One evening when she arrived, he asked her if she had been feeling well. Helen had found it impossible to hold his gaze.

"I get by," she had replied, somewhat lamely and had felt a tear prick behind her left eye.

"If you ever want a chat," he added, gently, "I'm always home, between seven and nine."

Helen didn't take the vicar up on his offer but his invitation hung in her mind. She continued to take her evening walks, to observe him sitting there. It was now late July and the evenings were long and light. One Sunday evening as she walked she heard laughter, cheers and curses throughout the village; it was the night, she realised, of the World Cup Final. People were enjoying the camaraderie of a TV event; something for which she had no feeling. As she passed blurred screens through open windows she suddenly thought of autumn, of nights drawing in, and realised at that time his curtains would be drawn too early for her to be able to observe him anymore, at least until the spring. She slowed as she came to the vicarage and stood there, looking in at him and this desk. It was ten past eight. She could read the time on his grandfather clock. And then he glanced up, before she had time to duck. To her momentary horror he stood up abruptly, opened the study door that led onto his back garden and called out to her. To her relief, he seemed delighted, not curious, to see her, standing there in the fading light, and the next thing she knew, they were sitting together on the garden chairs as the moon began to rise.

"Let me walk you home, Mrs Llewellyn," he urged her. It must have been close to ten o'clock. They had been sitting there together for nearly two hours, she realised, with surprise. Helen couldn't remember the last time someone other than Jane had spent so long in her company, talking of such small, inconsequential things.

"Come again," he said, as she bid him goodnight.

"Yes, I will," she replied.

"Oh, and by the way," he added, as if in afterthought. "Do call me John, if you prefer."

"Helen," she replied.

The following week Helen wandered past the vicarage on her way home from Jane's at half past seven. As she glanced his way she saw John sitting at his desk. He paused as he spotted her and beckoned her inside. She entered through the back gate as he opened the door and followed him into the study.

"Would you like a drink?" he asked with a broad smile, "It's at about this time I tend to mix myself a whisky and water."

"A glass of wine would be lovely," she replied, unable to suppress a wide smile.

"One moment," he replied happily and disappeared into the hall, humming.

Helen glanced around the lovely old, worn, panelled room, filled with books and files and old rugs. John's black spaniel, Petra, was asleep in front of the fire. It was only then that Helen noticed an old gilt mirror hanging on the wall above the desk. She moved towards the desk, sat down and looked up into the glass. From here she realised that you could see directly out of the back garden and onto the lane behind the house; her lane, the place where, so many times now, she had stood and watched him, apparently unobserved. She felt her heart leap into her throat as John reappeared, carrying a tray, and saw her, sitting there, in his place. He smiled as he put the tray down and came to stand behind her.

"Don't move," he said, very quietly, very gently. Then he placed an arm around her waist and moved closer so she could feel his face against the back of her hair. She wondered how she would ever breathe in the same way again.

"Sometimes when I'm working," he said as he moved his other arm around her waist and linked his hands, to draw her closer, "I look out and I watch the trees, swaying in the evening breeze, the world going by," his voice had taken on the same lilt as it had when he was reading a psalm, "And just occasionally, if I'm lucky, I see a badger, or a fox." He paused for a moment more and as she looked up into the mirror, she met his eyes. "And just occasionally," he added, very quietly, "If I'm very fortunate, I see you."

Pamela *Stevenage*

"This is what they had been missing. Some people had a soundtrack to their love lives. With a sort of grief, she realised that their lives were marked out by the foods they had never eaten."

Rachel Jackson

Pamela Stevenage
Rachel Jackson

The book had been the only present she had opened on Thursday. The other present had been a new iron, from Derek, but she had opened that on Wednesday night, because he'd needed his overalls doing and seen no good reason to wait. He was practical like that. The book had arrived on Thursday itself, her fifty-first birthday. Posted, wrapped in purple, Pamela had hoped it might be a box full of something exciting, but no, it was just a book. A cookbook written by a man, that Nigel bloke. This present had her daughter-in-law's handwriting all over it. Literally - she had scribbled inside - 'Happy birthday Pamela, love Sandra and Michael', her name first, as ever.

Pamela had called the same morning, thanking her so coolly that Sandra's voice had shrivelled slightly and she had hung up soon afterwards. Served her right. Hadn't they enjoyed enough Sunday lunches at her house to know she was hardly a novice? A bit of a natural even, in a solid, homely way. She had taken a quick look, just to see what sort of tarty soufflés the youngsters thought she should be serving up. Chicken, cheese, ice-cream, read the chapter headings. What was so difficult about that? Satisfied, she closed the book and put it in the sideboard drawer. Turn the other cheek, she thought. At least she had a new iron.

Derek would be back even later than usual. How many burst pipes and flooded loos could there be in one night? He was probably handing over his shift, checking in with Anne who co-ordinated the plumbers' call-outs. Divorced, newly-dieted, platinum-blonde Anne who had not yet hit forty…no. She could have got it wrong, he might be in the pub. There were so many matches it was hard to keep track. Derek adored football. He loved the build-up, the let-down, the bitching, the glory, the enemies, the cross of St. George, the betting, the red-and-yellow carding, the lot. He could be in some Red Lion or White Hart right now, watching yet another crucial game, dinner and Pamela far from his mind.

Best not phone him just yet. She could read her new present. The earlier indignation had seeped away: Sandra had clearly meant nothing by it. She was a bit testy these days, no one's fault. Her old friend Joan had raved about this Nigel when she had told her of the gift. Brilliant, so she said. Pamela liberated the book from drawer and began to read the recipes, starting with one for dauphinoise. At first she browsed them like they were simple lists, but by 9pm – still Derek-less – they read like love letters and finally, by the time she reached the muffaletta each one was a thriller.

As she devoured the stories, the words started to prod at her. This is what they had been missing. Some people had a soundtrack to their love lives; their own could be charted by food. No, that could not be right. With a sort of grief, she realised that their lives were more marked out by the kinds of food they had never eaten. Not just sushi, or suckling pig or caviar, but butternut squash and, there on page forty-eight, celeriac. So many years, so much food and none of it like this.

She had started it. Or perhaps they had: the snot-stained ones who once knew her as Pam Skeggs.

Her classmates had taken one look at her pink, shiny face and re-christened her Spam-and-eggs, Spam for short, from the very first day of primary. She had continued to feel insufferably porky right up until she had started dating Derek, which lead promptly into the lean years, the constant low-calorie diets the results of which, she could swear, had prompted him to propose.

Next came the shopping habits of an anxious bride gearing up for the long haul: all high-fibre bread and low-fat marge. Low-this, non-that, she had systematically trimmed away all of the flavour with most of the fat. With its flattened curves her newlywed body had threatened to become entirely the wrong sort of temple: purely functional, uninspiring and distinctly lacking in worshippers. After a while, Derek had quietly ignored her food obsessions in his own talented way, coming back from the pub more and more often via the chippy. Burger and chips, reheated steak and mushroom pie, cod and chips with a pickled egg and a battered sausage starter when he was feeling particularly expansive and good about life. She had soon got the hint.

Now, thirty-two years later and forty pounds heavier, she understood his appetites only too well. It was her job and she excelled at it. She had a PhD in all things Derek, a Manley Masters…but what of her? Had he not seen her lips and brow droop recently, her skin growing sallow, her touch become uncertain? Five months it had been, without one word of explanation. They had simply stopped doing it at all. No intercourse, no fondling, barely even a kiss. When she tried to raise the subject he gave her the look that drew the big black line between them. 'No go', the eyes said and so it had stayed, for five whole months.

As she read through the recipes, it began to occur to her that she could enhance this long education by browsing some new texts. He had seemed a funny sort at first, this Nigel, got over-excited about spuds in a way that Derek would think peculiar, but clearly a good man. You could just tell. And whenever you started a plan it was important to have a good man on board.

Derek had not slumped home until she was in bed, noisily depressed about the abject play and rubbish score. But the match must have finished hours ago. She chose not to listen, just as she ignored him the following night when he called home from a lucrative scenario involving a new kitchen and a spewing washing machine. She was far too busy in bed, marvelling at Nigel and his love struck prose.

Just take the way went on about cheese. There were one or two types she hadn't heard of, tally-something...but that wasn't it, he wasn't being fancy. He actually considered the excitement of unwrapping cheese, wrote about it melting 'sensuously', about oozing and flowing and generally got a bit hot under the collar until he came right out and said there were few sexier things you could put in your mouth. Cheese, that is. She had honestly never thought of it that way before. Derek was partial to a wedge squashed between ham and pickle in his packed lunch, or a hefty sprinkling on a jacket potato. But he only liked cheddar, or stilton at a push. This Nigel made it sound far more exciting than that. She had to be doing something wrong; they were clearly missing out. She lay the book on the pillow and went to the kitchen, returning with a scrap of paper. After a moment of deep thought and a quick check for spelling she added taleggio and fontina to her shopping list. Then she smiled and underlined them. No lightweight pleasures from this day on, forget frozen pies, saccharine joys no longer. She would sally forth with garlic press in hand... From now on salt in the Manley household would be Maldon's finest, her vinegar, balsamic, her chocolate, seventy per cent. Minimum!

The next morning, she awoke knowing that she had to thank Sandra properly. Coffee first, then an email – handwritten notes were nicer, but Michael would be delighted. He always complained that she should check her mail and become his friend on Facebook, whatever that might entail. She perched on the stool in front of their elderly PC. As she logged on, she felt a little surge of excitement. Forty-seven new messages! As soon as she clicked on her inbox, it became clear that she knew not a single sender. There were outlandish offers: miraculous diet pills, sex-aids for sale, luxury villas for rent, claims that she had won a Nigerian lottery and not one word from her son. He had told her to ignore all 'spam', for that was what it was called. The playground taunt had followed her right into the 21st Century. No wonder she hated email, even the rubbish had her name on it. She quickly bashed out a short thank-you to Sandra, including a suggestion that they come for lunch soon; the rest she would deal with later.

By the afternoon, Derek was installed in front of the TV. He was watching a replay of a vital match, apparently, not England, but another bunch whose victory was deemed important, or who needed a proper thrashing, or who had somehow ensured that England had gone home too early. This was just his warm-up viewing. There was to be a live match later that evening, kicking off at 7.30pm. This was no bad thing, she could feed him between matches, then leave him to watch the game whilst she bathed, did her legs and eyebrows and waited for him to come upstairs. Or she would check on him wearing just a towel, trailing perfume in her wake. It always used to work. But first a quick dash to supermarket, for the ingredients to make the Chicken with Vermouth, Tarragon and Cream and Best-Ever Mash. It was a recipe that could not fail – he liked chicken and loved his spuds, even though he could not translate that passion into poetry.

Returning home with two full bags, she found he hadn't budged.

"Alright, Love?" she cried from the hall.

"Alright," he replied, making no move to greet her. She set about preparing the ingredients as Nigel described. Doubt assailed her as she seasoned the chicken. Perhaps she should have gone for the pricier sort after all, he had gone on about it a bit…Too late now. She had well over an hour until kick-off, plenty of time to peel and chop, with Nigel by her side.

After a bit of faffing with the mash – she was just used to the peel-boil-pummel method – dinner was ready. The table had been laid with extra care, although she had changed her mind about adding a candle: far too obvious for her Derek.

"Come through, Derek," she cried. "It's ready." Derek appeared in the doorway, looking stricken.

"You can't possibly mean now, Pam?" She was carrying plates to the table as he spoke.

"Yes, it's only half six, you've got ages until it starts, love."

"Sweetheart, it's all the build-up now, that's the best bit," he pouted.

delicately dropped her finds into separate brown paper bags with a wary glance at the till. The old man in the corner showed no desire to intrude, just a gentle satisfaction in crunching almonds with his own teeth and creating piles of change on his counter.

Emboldened, she moved on to the wicker trays of pasta further inside. 'Farfalle', perhaps, or simply 'Linguine'. She would immerse it in boiling bubbles until perfectly al dente. She knew all about that. A delicious phrase, al dente, the actual feel of which she had repeatedly forgone to avoid another marital row about the omnipotence of the potato. An exuberant chef had once promised her that al dente held «resistance and a brief surprise of yielding», before cutting to the ads. She had never forgotten it: resistance, then yielding. She would drizzle it in olive oil until it was slippery and slick, and crush her garlic mercilessly in prolonged rites of preparation. Oils would be needed.

She walked down the aisle until she found the hoard: bottle upon jar of inexcusable extravagance, each costing twice the price of Derek's favourite lager. Yet not so alien after all, these translucent, stoppered ointments. She could confidently massage meat with truffle-infused oil. Go one shelf higher and Derek might warm her up with chilli and coriander oil and rub her down with mint and thyme. He might polish her thighs with walnut oil and open her up with sesame…Swallowing down a smile, she settled for some Extra Virgin and another one with sprigs of rosemary inside it. Best not get too carried away just yet.

She had been here before. Well, not here exactly, between the fresh 'Foccacia' and pungent mounds of cheese, but outside, looking in. This site had always held a fascination for her. The shop had been a foreign-language bookshop, not six months before. She had not dared then, had nothing to say to titles like Cien Años de Soledad or Les Liaisons Dangereuses. But she had browsed the stack outside, noted down the strange names and meant, one day, to see if they stocked English versions at WHSmith. The scrap of paper was probably still in her handbag, somewhere, but the moment had long passed. Other words offered themselves here now, like caramelle and dolcelatte and langoustine. She had a thing about foreign words, the way some women collected holiday souvenirs, or affairs with foreign waiters. She had flirted with a few French recipes years back, cutting the instructions from a series in Good Housekeeping. She had soon chucked them out, during one vigorous spring clean when she had realised she could not imagine a single occasion upon which her husband might countenance Enchaud de Porc à la Périgourdine .

But this: this was food that did not demand dressing up. Nigel might yet open up new ways between them. Derek might kiss her as he once had, not for the pedestrian smack of tongue and teeth, but to tease her taste buds and prime her palate for what was to come. He might knead her firmly, lick the salt from risen breasts. Or nibble at the kernel of her until her shell started to crack. He just might. They could stockpile all their zest for bitterer days and discover umami together.

Several large trugs of fresh herbs lay nearby, their scents soothed and encouraged. Greek oregano, flat-leaf parsley, marjoram, basil and bay. Pamela grabbed greedy handfuls of each, all thoughts of the house-keeping budget abandoned. She fought an urge to giggle. She could strew them around the bedside like rose petals, or even roll in them alone until their juice stained her skin like guilt. No, like lust. Or she could just scatter them over a leg of lamb. Either way, even her Derek could not possibly prefer any artificial sauce.

The bags rustled and rubbed as she walked. She would wear real nylon stockings. He might buckle to the living room floor and kneel to savour tastes long forgotten. He could, possibly, be moved to reconstruct the long, yet simple, recipe of her arousal upon a clean kitchen surface. It would be a feast like no other, quite unlike their salad days of chip butties and bolted pleasures. This was to be an act of premeditated desire.

As she moved nearer to the till she took in the display on the cold meats' counter. Black Forest, Parma and organic honeyroast hams, a red-brown, pink-purple parade of skilled carnal assaults. chorizo, kabanos and Ferrara salami, hot and hearty sounding islands, with all-male inhabitants. So much, so expensive, so very indecent. She took three types of ham and five different sausages – she would prepare him a novel platter which could be eaten in front of the footie. Derek might become angry at the cost and point an accusing kabanos at all the voided pots and jars. He might push her, furiously, against the clean kitchen surface and brandish the chorizo. He might just, irate, pull hungrily at her favourite knickers and, weary of all the brandishing, force the Ferrara between basting thighs and taste the sweet meat at the nape of her neck.

Nape. Another word they barely used. It was time to go.

Stopping only to grab a baguette and some honey, she made her way over to the old man, her basket grown heavy with good things. She paid, thanked him quietly and stepped out into the street. The sun was stronger than when she had entered, she took out her sunglasses once more, using them to push back her frizzing hair. She would let herself be dazzled. She would smile in the sun and walk with her bags of secrets and try to feel like 'a sort'.

She instantly regretted it. Just thinking of that word recalled the Anne situation (was it a situation already?) and reminded her that she, by wifely contrast, needed to buy a patio broom. Sad to end the trip with such a prosaic purchase, she hurried into the hardware store. The gardening area seemed dull after all those glistening meats and oils, but she still detected some charm. Real-bristle brooms, organic compost, scented gardener's soaps, old-fashioned rat poison. She looked again. Yes, there it was, in a lined hessian bag with a pink label. Just like pot pourri, or sweeties. She savoured the thrill that comes with finding dark things in pretty places. Lifting one package, she loosened the drawstring. Inside were dozens of harmless-looking little tablets, just one of which, according to the label, would kill a rodent stone dead. She brought it close and breathed in – no odour. A glance at her watch told her it was time to get going. She made her purchases and left.

Tonight was the end, at last: the World Cup Final. For countless millions it would be the night to decide the winner of the greatest sporting prize; a night to tell the grandchildren about in Utrecht or Seville. For Pamela it meant the end of one way of living and the start of something altogether different.

Derek was tightly coiled, so tense that he had declined invitations to the pub, the better to focus on the

12

Eliza Huffington *Cheshire*

*"She remembered her mo-
ther making the same mo-
tion, standing near the stove,
windows behind her open,
curtains billowing softly in
summer light. Like a ghost, the
memory floats through her
own kitchen, and out into the
warmth of the day."*

Jennie Walmsley

Eliza Huffington Cheshire
Jennie Walmsley

"If they ever write my obituary, I hope they mention the garden," Eliza Huffington thought as she opened the French doors onto the terrace. The rambling rose nodded in agreement, as she inhaled its perfume. The rose really was the best it had ever been in the twenty years since she'd planted it in that spring of "constructive grief". The bereavement counsellor had advised her to "do things", "make things" "grab at life positively". She'd gardened with a vengeance. And now it was lush and verdant, the fruit of all that pain, the way she'd wept and dug and planted. The rose was the queen of the terrace, clambering up the side of the cottage, as high as the thatch, in a tumbling waterfall of cream blooms that enveloped the cottage in delicate scent. She unhooked the secateurs from her hip and began to snip long stems, filling her basket. She wanted the house to be a sea of blossoms, so she could drown in their beauty. Eliza Huffington was determined to get what she wanted today. She often spent too much time bowing to others' desires. Today, she had decided, would be different.

Eliza Huffington was not naturally a decisive woman. Or rather, where she was decisive, she was also considerate, often putting the feelings or decisions of others before her own. It was characteristic of many women of her age who had just missed out on the invention of "the teenager", the pill, free love and

219

sexual liberation. Her generation had been raised by the previous one who had had to rebuild a fractured world. Eliza Huffington, or Eliza Gale, as she had been then, had not wanted to rock the boat. When she looked back on her life she wondered whether she might not have been more rebellious had Hitler not invaded Poland. Instead, her real defining strength had been realised in subsuming her own desires, blending in with her surroundings, not making a fuss nor demanding attention and not distinguishing herself in any particular way. It was a life which could be defined by letters: M&S, C of E, MOR, conservative (big and little c). Could one make an anagram of those, she wondered?

Eliza Huffington wasn't without a sense of humour. She could laugh at herself and take pleasure in mocking her own pettinesses, those small niggles that consumed many of her energies. She believed just as one was asked to draw oneself on the first day of school, so one came to think of oneself in the world, only minorly revised over the years "I am the sort of woman who always puts the milk back in the fridge." "I have a particular weakness for Thornton's Continental chocolates" "Coronation Street is one of my guilty pleasures". Her eldest son, Clive, had told her that such defining choices, whether, for instance, one preferred showers or baths, was often used in recruitment for jobs. It was called biometric testing. Eliza Huffington was a bath woman. And, she thought, as she deadheaded and snipped tendrils of rambling felicite perpetue, if she were to have to define herself as a colour it would have to be beige. Maybe cream. Even the colour image consultant she had seen the previous year (an unnecessary Christmas present from her daughter-in-law who was desperate) had found it difficult to categorise her. "You're a natural, Mrs Huffington," she'd said. "It's very rare I meet a woman so difficult to place on the colour palette. The blue of your eyes suggests a cool, winter personality, but your hair, though it's greying up now, still holds a surprising amount of its original hue. You must have been a wonderful auburn colour when you were young, which would put you on the summer spectrum. Really you're a wonderful..... chameleon individual. I think I'd have to recommend neutrals."

"Neutral" suggested absence. She preferred to think of herself as "classic", but "non-descript" would do just as well. Not that she minded too much: life has seemed easiest lived that way, and it had served her well and she had been, indeed was, happy. A marriage that had lasted "until death", two adult sons both making their ways in the world, a couple of grandchildren. An obituary based on her life up until today, Sunday 11th July, might be rather dull. "Time to give the editors of the parish magazine something to think about," she smiled to herself.

Because today Eliza Huffington was going to grab her life by the scruff of its neck and give it a good shake. She'd started early. Before dawn, a little after four. "Up with the lark," as her mother would have said. Her mother had been rather neutral too, until the dementia had transformed her into something technicolour. Something Eliza hardly dared to think about. A gibbering wreck who couldn't recognise herself in the mirror, who found it amusing to smear excrement around the bathroom, who would take pots of jam off supermarket shelves, spit into them and replace them where she'd found them. Eliza Huffington's mother, a pillar of the community and a bastion within the local WI, would have been mortified to see herself pull down her pants in the middle of the local village fete and wee near the cake stall. Or post dirty socks through letterboxes all around the village. The madness had arrived gradually, but it had arrived totally. There had been nothing left of the refined woman who had taught Eliza how to knit and garden and cook a meal so that vegetables and meat were ready at the same time. It had taken several months to realise that her mother was living off a diet of Ready Brek and plums, and that the tins and frozen packets that they bought together at their weekly combined supermarket shop were being quietly hoarded in the back shed or "liberated" in the village pond with papal ceremony (Eliza's mother chose to wear an outfit of purple as she threw bags of frozen peas into the pond reciting the Lords' Prayer in pig latin). At that point, Eliza Huffington had taken her mother into her own home. And she had seen the full indignity of a disease that melted your brain. The doctor had explained it to her as if the brain was a large sponge whereby the holes got larger "...until you're left with very little sponge, and mainly holes," he had shrugged and said helpfully.

That had been twenty years ago, the year the rose had been planted. Unfortunately, Eliza Huffington had seen the spread of the anti-sponge disease in two of her great aunts too, and it had not been dignified then either. The elder, Lucy, had embarrassed herself and the family in her final two years by attempting to seduce all the young soldiers stationed in the nearby barracks, despite the fact they were young enough to be her grandsons, and when that failed by attempting to bed any doctor, or in the end, nurse, who treated her. The other great aunt, after whom Eliza had been named, had ended her days tied to the bed and wearing a nappy. And that was in the days before disposables. Eliza Huffington wanted none of those indignities.

So, it had been necessary to make plans. Because she'd been getting a little forgetful recently, she'd made a list. Lists were organised. "Organised" was another word likely to feature in any description of Eliza Huffington. Although this list was rather more precious and private than those she normally made for shopping and such like. Because she couldn't risk it being discovered, she'd hidden in it in a locked drawer, the key to which she wore on a chain around her neck. That way the memory of the it wouldn't disappear in one of the ever growing sponge holes. She'd wake up in the morning, find a key hanging around her neck, and remember to unlock the drawer and consult the list.

Number 1 on the list: "Planting display". Since Eliza Huffington was a prodigious gardener, to the casual observer this would have seemed innocuous enough, though perhaps unnecessary to include on a "to do list." But this was no ordinary gardening. It required skill, speed, a degree of agility and, above all, stealth. Hence the pre-dawn alarm call. Eliza Huffington had gone to bed the night before fully clothed, dressed in a comfortable tracksuit, so that she could leave the house as soon as the alarm clock woke her. She'd tiptoed downstairs, although, of course, there was nobody else actually in the house with her, quietly picked up the prepacked rucksack from behind the back door, slipped on a pair of trainers and snuck out into the soft, grey light. She loved this time, the stillness just before dawn, when it was still technically night but the temperature fall had bottomed out, and the air began to hum with expectation. The ground was misted with dew, and the world was as silent as it would be for any part of the next twenty-four hours. Eliza Huffington stopped, closed her eyes and inhaled a long cold draught of air. Today was the day.

Eliza Huffington's back garden lay at a 90 degree angle to Alan Bower-Claridge's front garden. Alan Bowers-Claridge was a prominent member of the local golf club, with a loud voice and an inflated opinion of himself. His house, which he shared with his insipid wife Lynda was stupidly large for just two people, even ones with egos as big as theirs. His car was one of those four wheel drives that clogged up country lanes and threatened to squash small children, or old ladies, beneath its wheels with disdain. It had a number-plate with ABC 1. This area of Cheshire was stuffed with men like Alan Bowers-Claridge. People who thought that their accumulation of wealth through the sale of unnecessary merchandise was sufficiently good reason to allow them to disregard the views of others. Five years ago Alan Bowers-Claridge had decided it necessary to erect a huge garage-cum-gym-cum-entertainment centre bang up against the boundary he shared with Eliza. It overshadowed her garden, reducing the light and her planting options and limiting the areas of the garden where she could enjoy the evening sun. She had asked him nicely to position his folly elsewhere on his one and a half acre plot. He'd declined. Letters and missives and friendly, beige, neutral, polite chats had failed to shift him. She had objected to the local Planning department, and no doubt, because Alan Bowers-Claridge played golf with the right sort of men, men who had risen through local bureaucratic ranks to the dizzying heights of offices with their own doors, and sufficient incomes to join the golf club, her objections had been ignored. But one of Eliza Huffington's favourite phrases, perhaps even the motto which she would chose to ascribe to her life, and which, certainly from today took on an increased piquancy, was "Revenge is a dish best served cold."

She climbed nimbly over the low fence in the rear corner of her garden into his. There was a large section of his garden which faced the main road in the village and lay in front of the gym-cum-nightclub, from where she had calculated it would be impossible for her to be seen from Alan Bowers-Claridge's house. Not that he would see her, of course, given that he and his wife were three thousand miles away. "Got tickets for the Final," she'd heard him guffawing in the pub a few weeks previously, inhaling noisily through his nostrils and exhaling through his mouth in a nauseating bluster of slack cheeked "haw, haws". She had found herself hoping he'd choke on his vodka and tonic.

She stabbed her trowel viciously downwards, and scooped out a sod of dark soil. She'd chosen three words to match his pompous initials. She began with the only word of the three that she had ever uttered. Four letters. She'd considered putting "hole" on the end, but had decided the single syllable was sufficient. She'd been generous with the bulbs, allowing a good thirty per letter. Crocus goulimyi mani, in white, by mail order. A little early to be planting them now, but she didn't really have a choice, and she was fairly confident they'd bloom anyway. She covered them with a sprinkling of compost and a dribble of water, both carried in the rucksack.

Her second word for Mr Bower-Claridge was one her Northern mother-in-law had used frequently as a term of affection, though it seemed hugely inappropriate. Eliza had checked it out in the dictionary where it's first definition was "A disagreeable or contemptible person, esp a man or boy". But it could be a noun or a verb. She felt the solid red of the nasturtiums would help stamp the thought clearly. It was relatively easy to shake the seeds into the shapes of the letters. A capital B, lower case for the others. The "double g" was important to get symmetrical. A great sweep approximately four feet wide to get the full impact. She'd been practising sowing seeds in letter formation for a while now. She'd found she had a knack for it.

The final word, for the C, was middle English, according to the dictionary. Definitely a word she'd never uttered, not once in her whole life. Not when she'd given birth, and the medical profession had prodded and pushed around in the place. Nor in the extremes of passion (although she knew some couples did like to "talk dirty"). But she admired its brevity. Eliza Huffington liked to think of herself as a concise sort of woman. The village would be left in no-doubt about Alan Bowers-Claridge. An ABC of floral description.

She was back in her kitchen before the bells began calling the village's early risers to church. No one would have seen her. She made herself breakfast of tea, toast and a boiled egg which she ate in the kitchen listening to *Simon & Garfunkel* as she consulted the list. Number 2 : photographs. Eliza Huffington had recently mastered the art of digital photography. She'd entered a few in the recent fete competition, winning second place in the section devoted to "Village Landmarks". It had given her the excuse of shuffling about and snapping the oddest things from the strangest angles. Doorways and car registration plates. "Close ups of architectural features," she'd explained to anyone who'd asked. "You know, trying to get more interesting perspectives on the pub rather than a straightforward full frontal." People had liked to humour her, aware perhaps that she was becoming "eccentric". Maybe her son Clive had given people a hint of the family's genetic disposition. He was a doctor, after all, and couldn't resist being direct with people "Mum's got a form of Alzheimer's. It's been diagnosed early. Runs in the family. Could take years." Years till there's nothing but holes, and the sponge is rotted away. He doesn't say that to the locals, but that's what he means. Or maybe they're just tolerant in accepting older people's newfound hobbies. Miriam Astor won first prize at the fete with a most unusual angle of the vicar and she was new to photography too.

Eliza Huffington had managed to get enough evidence, anyway, to confirm what she'd suspected. It wasn't that she disapproved of adultery: far from it, in fact, had she been presented with the opportunity she often thought she might have indulged herself during the long drawn out fallow bit towards the end of Hugh's life. When he became incapable, and when she might have benefitted from some tenderness. Tenderness was what Karen Armstrong, the young woman who lived opposite required. Not the philandering of an ungrateful fool of a husband, who would see her off to her stressful job in the city at the crack of dawn on a weekday, whilst he, indulgent and indolent author that he was, retired to his bedroom to await the arrival of a string of young women whose bust measurements clearly outstripped their IQs.

The great benefit of digital photography,
of course, was that one needn't take anything to be
developed. Of course, that lent it the possibility of being
used in underhand and devious ways. Eliza turned
on the computer. She'd uploaded the photos over the
previous fortnight and sifted carefully for the ones that
were most revealing. A bit like putting together a cartoon
strip. Karen's car disappearing up the road. Her husband
answering the door in his dressing gown to a nubile
young thing. The upstairs curtains being closed. Eliza
had even managed to include her watch in one of the
photos just to heighten the drama. A bit like the way in
which hostage takers incorporated the front covers of
international newspapers in the films of their hostages to
indicate the immediacy of events. There was a tell-tale
England flag around. This year, this summer, this season.
Every day as Karen Armstrong drove the hundred and
fifty mile round trip to be at a deathly dull, thankless
desk in order to shift money around the world pointlessly,
this is what her husband has been up to. The man who
denies his wife's desire for children, who patronises her
in front of the entire village at drinks' parties repeating
the mantra that "We made a pact. Childlessness to
enjoy ourselves. It allows me to write. Karen's happy
making the money." Karen, whom Eliza Huffington had
encountered at the New Year's drink party, her face puffy
with tears and snot, desperate to have a child "before
it's too late, though he won't let me. His writing's too
important."

"So important," tuts Eliza as she clicks "print"
with the mouse, "He's prepared to spend it all, your
fertile youth, as he pursues his muse around the marital
bedroom."

228

Eliza Huffington sees herself as an avenging angel carefully sticking the series of pictures in to an album in chronological order. She's made the decision to catapult Karen into her future beyond the confines of this barren relationship. Eliza Huffington believes life's too short. She slides the album into a brown envelope addressed to Karen Armstrong at her work address. An anonymous incendiary device into the heart of the City.

She made a cup of tea. Slowly, indulgently, pouring hot water into the pot to warm it first, the way she learnt to as a child, circulating the water with gentle undulations of her arm. She remembered her mother making the same motion, standing near the stove, windows behind her open, curtains billowing softly in summer light. Like a ghost, the memory floats through her own kitchen, and out into the warmth of the day. She can hear children playing football down at the recreation ground, shouting tactics at one another. Clive and Paul were avid footballers when they were little. She thinks of them as they were then, knees scuffed, always on the move, orbiting around her. She misses them. "Always will," she thinks as she begins Task Number 3 of the day: Money-lending.

Eliza had never been particularly adept with money. It came with reassuring regularity through Hugh's salary at the bank. He'd made wise investments, which she didn't really understand, had bought lots of shares during Margaret Thatcher's era of privatisations, and dividends had continued to come with reassuring regularity ever since – even after he'd died. Not masses of it but enough to be comfortable. To shop at Waitrose without agonising, turn up the heating in the winter without worrying. But she knew not everyone was as

229

lucky. Over the preceding three months she'd been extracting largish sums of cash from the hole in the wall every time she went into town, bringing it home and putting it in a bag in her freezer. It was an old trick she'd learnt from her mother, in the days when she'd had all her marbles. "Keep some cash where the men are least likely to look," she'd said. In Mother's case it had been with the cleaning materials at the back of the pantry in a tin clearly marked with floor polish. Eliza didn't want Clive or Paul finding the cash. They'd only worry she was going to spend it unwisely. Given they were financially secure she didn't see why she shouldn't spend it unwisely. "On the dogs, for instance," she told herself. "Or a splurge in Las Vegas". She knew she was far too sensible for that. It was amusing to contemplate mad fripperies, but Eliza Huffington knew the value of cash. She knew how it could be hidden in secret places and liberated when necessary. Unlike shared bank accounts where joint signatories could spirit away figures and leave you bereft at the check-out.

Several months before she had rushed through Tesco to grab a pint of milk and found herself behind a neighbour at the checkout, one of the young women from the village. One often encountered other villagers in town: there'd be a civilised nodding or exchange of pleasantries. That day she had been unacknowledged by her neighbour from three doors down, a woman with two small children, her trolley over brimming with nappies and cereal boxes. Eliza Huffington had seen the humiliation rise in Jane Green's face as bankcard after bankcard was declined. Anger and scarlet embarrassment had flushed the young woman's face, accompanied by stuttering which made it apparent this wasn't unprecedented. Eliza had wanted to intervene, to help. She'd stepped in and offered to pay herself, but Jane Green had resisted. "It must be Mark's paycheque not gone through," she'd flustered, "Don't worry, I'll come back later." But Eliza had turned the remark around in her head afterwards. Paycheques might not have cleared, but that's why there were overdraft facilities.

Eliza Huffington had taken to watching out for that young woman. She'd noticed how she was punctual at the school gate but how she was prone to accidents. A fractured wrist here, and black eye there, concealed by sunglasses and a slightly too-loud laugh. All circumstantial, of course, but Eliza Huffington was a woman who liked puzzles, dot to dots, cryptic crosswords, Sudoku. Her answer to "three down" was an envelope containing five hundred pounds addressed to "Jane Green". She'd pop it through the letterbox a little later.

She organised herself a little after this. The cleaner would be in tomorrow to straighten things up properly, but she didn't like leaving things in a mess. She gathered a pile of dirty clothes and put them in the washing machine. She emptied bins around the place, folded and put away towels and wiped surfaces where they were dusty. She'd always been neat and tidy. In fact, it was one of the benefits of living alone that she could clear up and things would remain where she'd left them, tidily in their cupboards or where they'd been put on their shelves. She'd never mastered the art of living anarchically, which was what living in a household of men had meant for many years. Slowly, since their departure, she'd sorted things out, arranged systems that pleased her and simplified life, categorised laundry, organised cupboards. Eliza Huffington was

a woman who could locate candles and torches in the
event of a power-cut, knew where to find a needle and
thread at short notice, and always had the wherewithal
to make a meal for several people from the contents of
her cupboard. Not that she had much call for the latter,
now that Clive and is family had moved so far away, she
mused, as she took out a tin of tuna.

She examined the contents of the fridge. She
was peckish. She took out a bag of prawns out of the
freezer section for later. She pulled out the vegetable box.
There was a cucumber, some lettuce. A little high tea
then. Cucumber sandwiches, a slice of cake. A refined
English ritual with cup, saucer and teaspoon, sitting in
the living room admiring the summer garden. Revived,
she embarked on the next task. Number 4: Deliveries.

She made sure no-one saw her drop off the cash
at Jane's house. She knew the family would be out. Mr
Green played cricket religiously for the village team on
a Sunday and Jane and the children were expected to
attend and make tea. Eliza Huffington had observed that
he would often proceed to the pub whilst Jane was left
to put the children to bed. She hoped that this would be
the case tonight since the football was on, and that Jane
would, therefore, come home alone with the kids and
find the envelope. Eliza Huffington wanted her gift to be
anonymous.

She popped the envelope for Karen Armstrong
in the post-box as she passed. Walking out towards the
far edge of the village she came to the Manor House.
The people who owned it had always annoyed her.
They behaved as if they'd earned their luck, rather
than being merely descended from people who had
had the money to buy the pile in the late 19th century.

The Fishers had large labradors that they walked ostentatiously around the village, and allowed to defecate in the middle of footpaths without clearing up. Eliza Huffington had campaigned to have dog waste bins placed prominently around the village. There was no excuse. It was just laziness and bad manners. When she'd remonstrated recently with Mr Fisher, he'd huffed that he didn't have any bags with him, and that "..it rots quickly enough, anyway". She extracted the bag of prawns from her rucksack, pulled it open and began to throw its contents liberally around the manor's grand front lawn. It took only a couple of minutes and again she was fairly certain she had not been observed. She had achieved a surprisingly wide arc of prawns, and she suddenly understood the pleasure her mother must have derived from distributing frozen goods in this way. Perhaps there was less sponge left than she thought. Of course, the dogs might get to the prawns and eat them all she supposed, but she hoped that enough would hang around to create the right sort or aroma around the Manor, and, "Anyway," she told herself, "They'll rot soon enough."

She was home by six. She showered, changed into some comfortable clothes and poured herself a large gin and tonic before venturing into the evening sunlight to snip blooms from the clambering rose. It had been a satisfying day, nearly everything achieved that had been on her list. Smoke from barbecues drifted over the village with the sounds of televisions tuning into the build-up for the game. The drone of the vuvuzela, the South African horn, had been the defining sound of the summer. It was like a persistent bee, buzzing over the countryside, along with incessant television commentary. All that chatter over a game. Still, she hoped Clive and the children were enjoying themselves in South Africa. She'd encouraged them to go, to make a family holiday of it, even though it meant the children missing a fortnight of school. Sometimes rules needed to be broken. She realised that now.

She brought heaps of creamy flowers in to the kitchen, and filled every available jug and jar with their sweet scented stems. Then she went from room to room distributing them. She took a generous vase to her bedroom and put them on the bedside table next to the photo frames containing pictures of herself with Hugh, and the boys when they were younger. She fetched her glass and refilled it before lying on her bed. She opened the bedside drawer, took out ten tablets and swallowed them one by one with the tiniest sips from her glass. Then she sat back and addressed task number 6: correspondence.

She'd decided to keep them brief. One handwritten side of A4 for each of the boys. Democracy in parenting. She'd never discriminated between the two of them, although there were distinct differences. Clive had been more like his father temperamentally, more forthright, more demanding of the sunshine. He'd been a clever boy and had worked hard.

"Clive, I do hope you enjoyed the football, My Darling. Despite my best efforts, I found myself watching an awful lot of The Games, and wondering whether I might catch sight of you and the children in the crowds. It looked like such fun: the Africans know how to party, don't they? I hope you've had a wonderful time. I've missed you all, but you deserved a good holiday. I'm sure safari was wonderful too. I can imagine all the animals you saw.

Please don't be angry. I have my reasons for doing what I'm doing and you know some of what they are. I've always been

234

frightened of losing control, of getting it wrong and embarrassing you all. I want you to remember me as a dignified mother you could be proud of," (she hoped the anonymity of her day's tasks might help him with that). *"I have always been so proud of you and your brother. Give the children big kisses from me. All my love, Mum"*

She stroked the sheet of paper gently as if it was an infant's soft cheek. Keep it brief, keep it brisk. She checked her watch. The game had kicked off. Clive and the children would be watching. Much of the world, their faces pressed to television screens, living in the immediate moment. She gave a little sigh, a sip of gin and tonic, and started on the next letter,

"Paul, I've always thought being the younger child was hard. But you've done your own thing, and that was wise. I've loved both you and Clive equally, but differently. You are such different men and I know that has meant pain for you along the way. I know your father found it difficult to accept all the differences, but he was very proud of you both.

It has been wonderfully reassuring to me to see you settling down with Gary over these last three years. You make a lovely..." she hesitated over the next word, not *"unit"*, .."*family. I am sure he will continue to give you love and support over the coming years. I shall miss not seeing your garden grow, but be sure to take plenty of cuttings from mine. I like to think of my plants thriving with your tender care. Be happy. All my love, Mum"*

She put both letters in envelopes under the vase of flowers. They were such perfect blooms this year. She took one in her hand and manoeuvred herself a bit further down the bed, closing her eyes, gently breathing in the perfume from the petals. Through the open window she could hear the drone of the South African horns, mingled with the soft hum of bees and the reassuring murmur of people passing commentary to one another, the sound of friends chatting. She wondered which of the teams would win. All that energy, so much invested in a simple game. Something she understood, you'd never know the end to. As she drifted off to sleep there was a tremendous cheer that rose up from the gardens nearby, voices joined in unison and triumph that rolled up into the evening air and out over the green fields of England.

About the authors

Lucy Cavendish

I am a journalist and author. I write a column about my life in Stella magazine for *The Sunday Telegraph* as well as writing for many other newspapers; *The Observer, The Daily Telegraph*, *The Guardian*, the *Daily Mail* and *The Times*. I specialise in areas such as food, parenting and interviewing a variety of people. I have also been in various television documentaries about the history of the family and contribute to breakfast television programs. I am also on radio on a regular basis. With my other hat on, I am a novelist. I have three novels with Penguin; *Samantha Smythe's Modern Family Values*, *Lost and Found* and *Storm in a Teacup*. My next novel, *Jack and Jill*, also published by Penguin.

I live in the Chiltern Hills with my partner, my four children and my many animals.

At ten past eight, I am usually arguing with my eldest son Raymond about everything and nothing.

Miranda Glover

I am a writer and also work as an account director for a media agency. I am married with two children, Fen and Jessie, and own a mute black dog called Truffle. I have published three novels with Transworld; *Masterpiece, Soulmates* and *Meanwhile Street*. My current writing focus is on developing a short story programme for www.CWWC.co.uk and concentrating on shorter fiction. At ten past eight I may well be driving, working, speaking, cooking, cleaning, eating, drinking - but rarely writing or watching football.

Rachel Jackson

I first started writing short stories in 2001 for the *Erotic Review* under Rowan Pelling. Since then I have written for various women's magazines and been signed to Curtis Brown for a first novel. Publishing our first anthology, *The Leap Year*, was a joy and a revelation which has taken my writing in exciting new directions, as well as bonding me firmly with the other Queenbees. I live with my partner and his twins in a hamlet by the Thames, in surroundings that influence me as much as my Jamaican-Nigerian roots.

My ideal ten past eight moment would be spent sitting by the river, in the dying days of summer, with said partner, children and dogs, enjoying a large glass of Syrah as the sun sinks over the south Oxforshire Downs.

Jennie Walmsley

I have worked as a journalist, media trainer and consultant for many years. Writing is a wonderful antidote. As well as writing fiction, I love gardening and swimming and (often) being with my partner and three kids.

At ten past eight, I've got a glass of wine and I'm chopping onions.

Epilogue

It's a beautiful autumnal morning; sharp sun, crisp air with the promise of winter. I open the window and watch the leaves floating through the air like little golden goddesses. I'm relishing my solitude, husband away and the semi-flown children in semi-flown mode. Last night was pure pleasure, Greek salad, a glass of wine, a double bill of *Mad Men*, a soak in the bath and the final perfect pleasure, lying in bed with a good read. It was well past 2.00am when I turned the light out.

Ten Past Eight is an eclectic and diverse mix of compelling stories. All include two components; an enticing saucy edge and just a passing pointer to the world with which I and my family have more than a passing relationship – football. Pop this book in your bag and you can savour each story as a literary quickie. I met Miranda Glover and Lucy Cavendish when I went to two of their seminars at *The Henley Literary Festival*. I was intrigued to learn about *The Contemporary Women Writers' Club* and their soon to be launched programmes. It's a great concept which will inspire pockets of writers across the country to come together to collaborate and critique each other's work.

I introduced myself and soon my connection with writing and the world cup came to light. They invited me to contribute a novice ten past eight story to the collection, with an authentic world cup twist. It's an example of what they are hoping you as emerging writers might achieve if you get involved in *The Contemporary Women Writers' Club* (www.cwwc.co.uk) and learn, like me, to start finding your own literary voice.

Flora *The Final*

"Flora's wardrobe is a mix of vintage and Oxfam, most of which she customises herself with her ancient sewing machine. Today's outfit is colourful and quirky, it isn't a look she cultivates, it's just who she is."

Vanessa Hoddle

Flora Italy
Vanessa Hoddle

Flora wriggles her toes and stretches; she listens to the usual hum of activity outside. Home is a one bedroom flat in Bethnal Green. She glances around at the comfortable chaos and then scans the walls at her unsold paintings. She emerged from Central St Martin's two years ago and is endeavouring to make a name for herself. This year she's taken a stand at the Affordable Art Fair, which she can't really afford. She's banking on her prized painting, *The Cheetah* selling to cover her costs.

Until now living day to day as a painter has only been possible because of Flora's godfather. Her father's best friend has been her friend and mentor, offering emotional and financial support, ever since the loss of her own dad. In fact he would have done more to include her in his life but until now she has actively shied away from his world; she dislikes the glitz and the apparent madness. She also despises the way the press alternately revere then attempt to destroy his reputation.

Until now. Flora's godfather is taking his team to the World Cup Final and Flora understands that to not accept his invitation to go along would be unforgivable. And anyway, she is excited.

The itinerary arrived several days ago. Lying on the matt with grand reverence, its thick envelope and unmistakable logo appeared regal amongst the bills and junkmail. No detail in the agenda was left unattended,

251

no minute without a purpose. She had been invited to join wives, partners and their families for three days of organised luxury.

Flora showers and dries, then assembles her clothes for the journey. She twists her hair up and secures it with what she has to hand, a pencil. Flora's wardrobe is a mix of vintage and Oxfam, most of which she customises herself with her ancient sewing machine. Today's outfit is colourful and quirky, it isn't a look she cultivates, it's just who she is. She's a take it or leave it kind of girl. On impulse she grabs her portfolio of sketches and some photos of her finished work and pops them in 'Harold', an old doctor's bag which acts as her hand luggage. All of Flora's precious possessions are allocated names, Harold after her grandfather, Gertrude, her bike, because it looks like a midwife's bike and that's a perfect name.

She peers out of the window in time to see a sleek black Mercedes draw up, then bounces her suitcase down the stairs and bangs the front door shut. With an expansive smile she hands her bag to the driver and jumps in the car. Within minutes she's picking his brains, assembling as much information as possible about the England team. He gladly volunteers his opinions and she wonders if all these wannabe managers would agree with her godfather's decisions. She listens with half an ear whilst idly glancing through a *Hello* magazine, left by the previous passenger. Endless glossy, immaculate figures stare back. This issue is littered with the WAGS with whom Flora suddenly realises she is about to spend the next three days of her life.

The early morning traffic has cleared and the car effortlessly glides towards the airport. As they pull up at the departures lounge photographers gather round the Mercedes expectantly. After a quick slick of red lipstick to her, Angelina Jolie lips, her one concession to make-up, Flora pulls the pencil from her hair and the nearly-dry chestnut waves tumble half-way down her back. She decides it's time to have some fun, so steps out of the car with a flourish and sashays towards the lounge, happily posing while the photographers click furiously. A bodyguard arrives and she is reluctantly rescued: when they realise she can't be attached to a footballer it will be bit of a disappointment. She knows she looks a million miles away from the waif-like, coiffed WAGS waiting inside.

Moments later Flora's being relieved of her luggage and passport and is given her boarding card. Then she finds herself in the lounge with throngs of people and a glass of champagne in her hand. A quick glance confirms there's an army of WAGS standing around in Blahnik by Vuitton. Next to her is a shining, perfect petite blonde and she introduces herself as Louise with surprising warmth. Flora recognises her from *Hello* and discovers to her relief that they are sitting next to each other on the plane.

She confesses to Louise that she's looking forward to the next ten hours of pure unadulterated luxury of private, first class travel. After placing their hand luggage in the overhead lockers, Harold looking a little incongruous next to the latest little Louis Vuitton, Flora sits in the middle and Louise pops her tiny frame in the aisle. Soon they are swapping details of their day to day lives. Louise is a young mum with two children; she's taking private Spanish lessons and would love to go to the local college but feels a little chained by her circumstances. Within days of starting a Spanish course the press would begin another rampage about their obsession with her husband's possible transfer from his London club to Spain. It's evident that whilst she lives in a lap of luxury, her life is a little lonely and isolated. Clearly she's intrigued with this carefree confident girl beside whose life couldn't be more different from hers.

Flora shows Louise her portfolio and she spends a long time devouring the sketches and looking at the photos of the final pieces. Clearly art is a passion they share. To her delight, Louise says her favourite is *The Cheetah*.

Flora snoozes happily and a few hours later is jolted awake by the captain saying "ten minutes to landing". With the same precision as on arrival at the airport in London, the passengers are ushered through departure. Press and fans are outside so the organisers and bodyguards bustle everyone onto the coach.

The hotel is even more opulent than Flora has imagined. She knows she'd need to sell a lot of paintings before she could ever travel in this style from her own purse. Finally she steals a few minutes to herself and goes for a quick stroll outside the hotel. A fan broaches her and offers an extortionate amount for a ticket, very quickly a bodyguard moves him on – she's been totally unaware of her protector and it is all slightly unnerving.

That night when her godfather calls, he explains that security has to be that tight. Flora tells him that there is unrest 'in the camp'. The WAGS are unhappy that her godfather has refused any visits from the footballers, and only half an hour on the phone this evening but he's totally unperturbed. Flora wishes him all the love and luck in the world and they say goodnight.

There's a distinct change in atmosphere when everyone gathers for a pre-match drink prior to the coach journey. Apprehension is palpable and it is tinged with both fear and excitement. Despite herself, Flora is being pulled in and she feels a knot of worry for her godfather. This man who is her rock is fallible and she has never considered the pressure he's under before.

As he forewarned, security is very tight and timing is crucial. Motorcycles surround their coach as they journey through the city streets. With perfect timing the two coaches merge and the wives, partners and family follow the players. Twenty two motorbikes surround both coaches and as Flora glances down at the man with his black helmet, it strikes her that perhaps her mum has a point, that careering around London on Gertrude without a helmet is a tad dangerous. As they drive through another set of red lights like visiting dignitaries, that thought is confirmed. Then it is the moment at last: they enter the stadium. Flora's chest feels tight. Clutching her ticket she reaches her seat. Glancing around two rows behind her she sees Louise. There's the gleaming smile again and she's waving an envelope. It's passed down to her. They mouth to each other to meet after the game. The tension is mounting; on the pitch the Italian opera singer is filling the stadium with his extraordinary voice. Flora fumbles with the envelope, a cheque for £5,000 falls out and a little note – *For the Cheetah, I love it! Louise*. Flora fells overwhelmed. She turns and blows a kiss, and Louise smiles back. The excitement is mounting. Her neighbour asks for the time and brings her back to the moment. She looks at her watch but it's still on English time, says ten past eight. Even so it's clear that there's no time to go now, the game's about to begin.

About Vanessa Hoddle

Ever since I was in my twenties I have kept a diary on an ad hoc basis which has seen me through the birth and raising of my three lovely children, Olivia 26, Toby 22 and Amelia 18. I have been an air stewardess and I have worked discreetly as a private stylist – always indulging my passion for cooking and collating ideas from travels around the world.

With Olivia now being of the age that I was when I had her, I take great delight in seeing her emerge from the chrysalis as an actress. I now feel that the time is right for women like me to pursue our own dreams. In my case, that means writing in whatever form it takes. I am immensely grateful for this chance to get my words into print for the first time.

Thank you

We would like to thank everyone who has had a part in the creation of our new collection. The design process has been very collaborative and lots of talented people have given generously of their time, including creative direction from Michael Agar, cover illustration by Richard Burgess and design by Sarah Allen, Charlotte Morgan and Anna Fidji. We thank you all very much.

Lightning Source UK Ltd.
Milton Keynes UK
172220UK00001B/4/P